THE DARK RIVAL

The epic begins . . .

STAR WARS®
EPISODE I
THE PHANTOM MENACE™
By Patricia C. Wrede
Based on the screenplay and story by George Lucas

See Episode I through their eyes . . .

STAR WARS®
EPISODE I
JOURNAL

Anakin Skywalker
Queen Amidala

. . . and more to come

Before there was *The Phantom Menace*, there was . . .

STAR WARS®

JEDI APPRENTICE

#1 The Rising Force

#2 The Dark Rival

. . . and more to come

STAR WARS

JEDI APPRENTICE

The Dark Rival

Jude Watson

LUCAS BOOKS

SCHOLASTIC INC.

New York Toronto London Auckland Sydney
Mexico City New Delhi Hong Kong

No part of this publication may be reproduced in whole or in part, or stored in a retrieval system or transmitted in any form or by any means, electronic, mechanical, photocopying, recording, or otherwise, without written permission of the publisher. For information regarding permission, write to Scholastic Inc., Attention: Permissions Department, 555 Broadway, New York, NY 10012.

ISBN 0-590-51925-5

Cover design by Madalina Stefan. Cover art by Cliff Nielsen.

12 11 10 9 8 7 6 5 4   9/9 0/0 01 02 03

Printed in the U.S.A.
First Scholastic printing, June 1999

THE DARK RIVAL

CHAPTER 1

K-7, Core 8. Core 7. Core 6. Core 5. Narrow. Pressure. Trapped.

"Yes, Qui-Gon. I can do it. I will do it."

He knows it is wrong. He must stop it. But he can't fight this power. He sees the broken circle. The circle that brings the past to the future, yet does not meet. He must make the circle meet. He must . . .

Qui-Gon Jinn woke with a start. As always, he knew exactly where he was as soon as he awakened. Dreams never hung on him, clouding his mind.

Even a nightmare had only served to sharpen his senses. The room was dark, but he could make out the edges of the window in the darkness. Dawn was near. He could hear Obi-Wan Kenobi's quiet breathing on the sleep-couch next to him.

They were quartered in the guest chamber of the Bandomeer governor's official residence. He had come to the planet on a routine mission that had suddenly turned non-routine, all because of a single line written on a piece of paper.

The message had brought the nightmare. He'd had the same one for three nights running.

Qui-Gon's hand fell on his lightsaber, placed so that it was in easy reach in case of intruders. Within the blink of an eye, he would be standing, ready to fight.

But how could one fight a dream?

K-7, Core 5. What could the words and numbers mean? K-7 could be a charted but uninhabited planet, or a star system. But why did he have such a sensation of being trapped? Who had said, "I can do it"? And why did he rage against the words, why did he feel helpless despair as he heard them?

The only thing that was familiar to him was the image of the broken circle. It filled him with dread.

He thought it was in the past. All of it. Then, upon his arrival on Bandomeer, he was handed a note. It welcomed him to the planet, and it was signed *Xanatos*.

Jedi are taught to value dreams, but not to trust them. Dreams can confuse as well as illuminate. A Jedi should test a dream much as he tests unstable ground. Only when he's sure of his footing should he move on. Dreams can be random energy, nothing more. Some Jedi see things in dreams, and others do not.

Qui-Gon rarely had the gift and preferred not to dwell on dreams. He managed to push dreams away in the daylight. But at night, it was harder. If only he could ban his nightmares, and memories. Then they would not be able to haunt him so.

He had been all over the galaxy, from the Galactic Core to the Outer Rim Territories. He had seen many things that pained him, and many things he wished he could forget.

Now his worst pain, his worst regret, had caught up with him at last.

CHAPTER 2

Qui-Gon was the one who discovered Xanatos, the one who took the midi-chlorian count and brought the child back to the Jedi Temple.

He remembered the look on Crion's face as his only son was taken from his home planet of Telos. Crion was the wealthiest man on Telos, but he knew, despite all his riches, he could not offer Xanatos what Qui-Gon could. He could not deny his son. Qui-Gon saw the heartbreak on the man's face, and he hesitated. He asked one last time if Crion was sure of his decision. Slowly, Crion nodded. The decision was final. Qui-Gon would take Xanatos to be trained as a Jedi.

If only Qui-Gon had listened more closely to his own hesitation. The decision to take the child would have been different. All of their lives would be so different. . . .

Qui-Gon swung his legs over the side of the sleep-couch. He crossed to the window and pushed aside the heavy curtain. He could just make out the mine towers in the gray light. The Great Sea of Bandomeer was a black void in the distance.

Bandomeer consisted of one huge land mass and one enormous sea, which divided the planet in half. All of it was owned by mining companies. There was only one city — Bandor, where the governor's quarters were located. But even the city was dotted with mining operations. The air was a sheet of dull gray, filled with drifting black specks.

It was a desolate world. The majority of Bandomeer's mines were controlled off-planet. None of the enormous riches made it back to the native Meerians. Even the official residence of the governor was shabby and ill-furnished. Qui-Gon's fingers ran along the edge of the curtain. The fabric was beginning to fray.

Obi-Wan stirred in his sleep. Qui-Gon turned to watch the boy, but Obi-Wan slept on. Qui-Gon let him. Today would mark the start of their separate missions on Bandomeer. Although

Obi-Wan's mission wasn't dangerous, it would test the boy. All missions tested Jedi skills, even the ones that appeared easy. Qui-Gon had learned this long ago.

He and the boy had just been through a dangerous and unexpected journey together. They had fought side by side and stared death in the face. Yet he couldn't feel close to Obi-Wan. There was still a part of him that hoped Yoda would call the boy back to the Temple for reassignment.

Qui-Gon forced himself to be honest. The reason he couldn't feel close to Obi-Wan was because he wouldn't allow himself to. Certainly, the boy had impressed him on the journey here. It had been a rough transport, filled with tensions. Obi-Wan had learned to hold his tongue and his temper in situations where Qui-Gon had been certain he would lose his calm.

But Qui-Gon also knew that Obi-Wan was still too blindly guided by ambition and anger. Those were the two qualities that had led to Xanatos' undoing. Qui-Gon couldn't get involved in such a situation again. He knew how treacherous it could be to rely on an apprentice.

So he would keep his distance from young Kenobi. Soon Obi-Wan would be sent to observe the Agricultural Corps work on the planet. Thanks to mining, Bandomeer had been stripped of many natural resources. The great mines took up many square kilometers; when the land was depleted, the mine was closed and left the area barren. It was no longer useful for farming. Food was shipped in from other worlds.

It was a precarious situation that the local government was working to change. It had plans to restore and reclaim the land and vast ocean. The Agri-Corps was helping in that endeavor by replanting large areas and enclosing them to form what the government called "Enrichment Zones." Obi-Wan would be sent to the largest zone to help.

Qui-Gon's mission was less clear-cut. He had been called on by the Jedi Council to act as a Guardian of the Peace at the local government's request. Qui-Gon still wasn't certain of the specifics. Most of the people on Bandomeer were imported to work in the mines. They worked, saving as much as they could in order to transport off-planet as soon as possible. That was why the government of Bandomeer had such trouble instituting change. Everyone, even the natives, wanted to leave the planet as soon as they were able. No one truly cared what happened to Bandomeer.

But recently, that had begun to change. The Meerians had become partners with the immigrant Arconans. The two groups had formed a cooperative mine. All of the profits were shared equally.

Some miners had already switched over from the main mines, owned by the mighty Offworld Corporation. Qui-Gon had a feeling that the reason he'd been called by the Bandomeer government was because of this. Offworld never took well to those who encroached on its turf.

The landscape outside was lighter now. Streaks of a deep orange sun licked at the tall mining towers like tongues of flame. Still fighting the grip of his nightmare, Qui-Gon watched Bandor come to life. Lights came on in the narrow streets. Workers headed for the mines. Night workers wearily trudged home. Qui-Gon's thoughts returned to Xanatos' surprise message:

I have been looking forward to this day.

The message included a small drawing of a broken circle next to Xanatos' name — there was a gap where the ends should meet.

It was a reminder to Qui-Gon. A taunt. Xanatos had a scar on his cheek in that form. Qui-Gon meditated on the message again, letting all the possible implications come to him. He could be walking into a trap. Or Xanatos could be playing a game with him. He could be galaxies away right now, smiling at the idea that he made his former Master shudder in fear at the sight of his name.

That *would* be something Xanatos would do: confuse Qui-Gon, slow him down, make him interpret a situation badly, all because Qui-Gon assumed Xanatos was involved. Xanatos was clever, and often used that cleverness to concoct cruel games.

Suddenly, Qui-Gon wished the message had been a game. A childish taunt.

He did not ever want to meet Xanatos face-to-face again.

CHAPTER 3

Obi-Wan Kenobi woke, but did not stir. Keeping his eyelids almost closed, he stole a glance at Qui-Gon. The Jedi Master stood at the window. His back was to Obi-Wan, but the boy could tell by the tension in his muscular stance that Qui-Gon was brooding again.

Obi-Wan itched to ask Qui-Gon what he was thinking. His mind had been jumping with questions since they'd landed on Bandomeer. What had changed Qui-Gon's mood from serenity to agitation? Was Qui-Gon going to include him on the Jedi's mission as Guardian of the Peace? Had Obi-Wan proved himself a worthy candidate for Qui-Gon's apprentice?

Since leaving the Temple only a few days before, Obi-Wan had been shot at with blasters and strangled by a Hutt. He had tangled with Togorian pirates, fought off giant flying draigons, and piloted a huge transport vessel through heavy laser cannon fire. But apparently, he had not done enough to impress Qui-Gon.

If only he could hold on to the serenity he had been taught at the Temple. He knew that as a Jedi pupil, he should accept what life offered him with calm. But his position was so maddening! He had completed his Temple training, but no Jedi Knight had chosen him as an apprentice. On his thirteenth birthday, it would be too late. And that was only three weeks away!

It seemed that his destiny was to be a farmer, not a warrior or peacekeeper. Obi-Wan had thought he had begun to accept this, but it was hard. He couldn't help but feel that a different path was his destiny.

Obviously, Qui-Gon didn't think so. Although Obi-Wan had saved the Jedi Knight's life, Qui-Gon acted as though Obi-Wan had merely done him a friendly gesture, like helping him fix a broken lock. Obi-Wan's loyalty and dedication were received by Qui-Gon with polite acceptance, nothing more.

Qui-Gon turned slightly, and Obi-Wan studied his profile. The Jedi Knight's worry and preoccupation filled the room along with the growing light. It had begun after Qui-Gon had received that note. Qui-Gon had passed it off as a greeting from an old acquaintance. But Obi-Wan didn't believe him.

Still gazing out the window, Qui-Gon suddenly spoke. "You should dress. It's almost time for the meeting."

Obi-Wan sighed as he threw back the light blanket. He hadn't moved one muscle, yet Qui-Gon had known he was awake. The Jedi Knight was always at least two steps ahead of him.

Why didn't Qui-Gon tell him what was wrong? Was it the message, or was Qui-Gon tired of Obi-Wan?

Obi-Wan wanted to blurt out the question. But one of the Jedi's most serious rules was not to cross-examine a Master. Truth can hold great power. Therefore the decision to share it must be weighed. Only the Master could decide on revelation or concealment, according to the greater good.

For once, Obi-Wan was glad of a rule that restrained him. He was afraid of the answer to the question he wanted to ask.

Obi-Wan followed Qui-Gon into the governor's receiving room. He was surprised and encouraged that Qui-Gon had invited him to the meeting. Perhaps it meant that the Jedi was reconsidering whether to take him on as apprentice after all.

Obi-Wan was expecting a lavish chamber, but there was only a circle of cushions on a bare stone floor. Bandomeer could not afford to impress guests.

SonTag, the governor of Bandomeer, entered the room. Her silver hair was cropped in tufts in the Meerian style. Her dark gaze calmly rested on the Jedi. Like all of the Meerians, she was small. Obi-Wan towered over her. The Meerians' small stature had made them great miners.

She held out both hands, palms up, in the Meerian way. Qui-Gon and Obi-Wan repeated her gesture.

"Greetings and welcome," she said softly. She indicated the younger woman to her left. The younger woman's cropped hair was also pale silver, and her silver eyes blazed at them across the room. Although she was standing quietly, her energy seemed to send a vibration through the air. "This is VeerTa. She is the leader of the Home Planet Mine."

The Jedi greeted VeerTa in the same fashion. They had been briefed about her. She was a fierce patriot who had been instrumental in forming the Home Planet Party. The party goal was to replant the once fertile fields of Bandomeer, as well as control its resources. The first step was to end dependence on off-planet corporations for financial support. To that end, VeerTa had gone into partnership with the Arconans in the cooperative mine.

SonTag indicated the cushions that the Jedi should sit on and took her own seat. Slowly, SonTag and VeerTa's cushions rose in the air so that they were at eye level with Qui-Gon and Obi-Wan.

"I've asked VeerTa to join us today because we are both confused by your presence," SonTag began. "Although we welcome you, we must admit we are surprised. We understand that the Agri-Corps has requested help. But we did not."

Qui-Gon looked startled. "But the Temple received an official request from the government of Bandomeer for a Guardian of the Peace. I have the documentation."

"I'm sure you do," SonTag said firmly. "But I did not send it."

"This is very strange," Qui-Gon murmured.

"Nevertheless, we are glad you are here," VeerTa said crisply. "We have our doubts that Offworld Corporation will allow us to operate freely. Let us just say that the corporation has a history of making competition disappear."

"I've seen how they operate firsthand," Qui-Gon responded. "I have to agree."

Qui-Gon's voice was neutral, but Obi-Wan knew how deeply the Jedi disapproved of Offworld practices. On the journey to Bandomeer, Obi-Wan had been shocked at how openly Offworld used intimidation, threats, and outright violence to keep control of their employees. Jemba the Hutt had deprived a group of Arconans of the precious substance that kept them alive. He offered a brutal choice: to work for Offworld, or die. He even laughed in their faces as they grew too weak to move.

"Then you'll understand why we'd like to have a Jedi representative at our first meeting with Offworld," VeerTa said. "Your presence will ensure that everyone plays fair."

Qui-Gon bowed. "I'll be happy to contribute what I can."

Excitement rose in Obi-Wan. Obviously, the meeting ahead would be important. The future of a planet was at stake. Plus, since the Home Planet group was in league with the Arconans, he would probably get to see Clat'Ha and Si Treemba again. He'd made friends with both of them on the journey to Bandomeer. Surely Qui-Gon would want him present at the meeting.

"My companion will be traveling to the Eastern Enrichment Zone," Qui-Gon said, indicating Obi-Wan. "Can you arrange transport for him?"

Obi-Wan barely listened to SonTag's agreement. Stirrings of anger began to flutter underneath his frustration. While Qui-Gon would be involved in saving a planet, he'd be watching plants grow! He would be a farmer, after all.

He'd held on to a hope that after their adventures reaching Bandomeer, Qui-Gon would cancel Obi-Wan's original mission. Obviously, Qui-Gon still didn't believe he could become a Knight. He would send him off to farm before taking him as a Padawan!

Obi-Wan struggled with his anger. Master Yoda had told him that often anger wasn't about another person, but about himself. "Close your mouth and open your ears, you must," Yoda had said. "Then hear what your true heart is seeking, you will."

Well, right now his true heart was seeking to scream out his frustration.

Qui-Gon extended his hands, palms up, then flipped them over, palms down. It was the farewell gesture of the Meerians. SonTag and VeerTa repeated the gesture. Nobody seemed to care what Obi-Wan did, so purposefully, he did not acknowledge their parting.

Obi-Wan's lack of courtesy was a severe infraction for a Jedi pupil. But Qui-Gon didn't say a word as they walked through the residence halls and out the main door.

The air chilled Obi-Wan's flushed cheeks as he and Qui-Gon paused on the steps. Obi-Wan waited for the older Jedi to reprimand him. Then he could tell Qui-Gon how he wanted to remain in Bandor. He could line up his reason;

he could argue that Qui-Gon needed his support.

"Those seeming not to notice you usually do," Qui-Gon said, looking out into the distance. "They choose not to show it. Or they have greater concerns on their minds. It is no reason for discourtesy."

"But I —"

"I see that your discourtesy sprang from anger," Qui-Gon continued. His voice was soft and low, as it usually was. "I will ignore it."

Angry words sprang to Obi-Wan's mind. *If you're choosing to ignore it, why are you mentioning it?*

Qui-Gon looked at Obi-Wan directly for the first time. "You will not, under any circumstances, intervene in any situation regarding my mission, or take any action, without contacting me."

Obi-Wan nodded.

Qui-Gon's gaze swept the mine towers of Bandor. "Things are rarely what they seem," he murmured.

"That is why I wish to —" Obi-Wan started.

"Come," Qui-Gon interrupted sternly. "Let's get your things. You must catch that transport."

He strode off briskly. Obi-Wan followed more slowly. He saw his chance of being a Jedi Knight dissolve in the cold, gray air.

CHAPTER 4

Xanatos was not an easy student. Though he was very young when he left Telos, he remembered that he had come from a powerful family on a powerful planet. He used the information to try to impress the other students, most of whom were from less privileged backgrounds.

Qui-Gon was patient with this fault, he considered it a childish failing that would disappear with time and teaching. When they first arrived at the Temple, most of the students still missed their families and home planets. Many of them spun tales about their backgrounds or retold remembered stories. Xanatos really wasn't that different, Qui-Gon told himself. And the boy made up for his snobbery with a genuine desire to learn and an excellent aptitude for Jedi *skills. When the time came, Qui-Gon chose Xanatos as his Padawan learner.*

After seeing a simmering Obi-Wan off on his transport, Qui-Gon went for a walk. His mind mulled over the morning's meeting. Who had fabricated the request for Jedi intervention in Bandomeer affairs? If it was Xanatos, what was his reason? Had he lured Qui-Gon into a trap?

Qui-Gon pondered the questions, but came up with no answers. If there was a trap ahead, he couldn't see it. He could hardly confess to SonTag that he couldn't help because of a mysterious figure from his past who might still hold a grudge. The only thing he could do was proceed. The mission on Bandomeer was real. SonTag and VeerTa needed help.

SonTag sent word to Qui-Gon that the meeting with Offworld would take place at the Home Planet Mine. At the scheduled time, Qui-Gon headed out of his quarters. He found SonTag herself heading toward him down the hall.

"I'm glad I caught up with you," she told him. "We've changed the location of the meeting. I think it's better for both parties if we meet in a neutral place. Maybe if there's an official tone to the proceedings, everyone will be more polite." SonTag grimaced. "At least that's what I hope."

"I hope the same," Qui-Gon agreed. He shortened his long stride to match SonTag's.

In the receiving room, VeerTa stood waiting. She was wearing the gray-blue unisuit of a miner, along with an impatient look.

"This meeting is a waste of time," she told Qui-Gon brusquely. "Offworld will make us pretty promises and then break them."

"I'm here to ensure that they don't," Qui-Gon answered. He liked the fiery VeerTa. He hoped the meeting would go well for her sake, and for Bandomeer's.

The door opened, and Clat'Ha, the Human manager of the Arconan Harvest mining operation, entered. Qui-Gon greeted her with a bow. She returned it, her vivid green eyes giving him a warm glance. They had been allies on the ship to Bandomeer; he hoped they would remain so here.

They waited for several minutes, but the Offworld representative didn't show up. Since Jemba the Hutt was killed during the journey to Bandomeer, nobody knew who the new representative would be. Offworld's power structure was clouded in mystery. No one even knew who its leader was.

Finally, an annoyed SonTag gestured at the cushions.

"We might as well start the meeting," she said. "If they're trying to intimidate us, I'm not going to fall for it."

Everyone took their seats. The cushions made height adjustments so that everyone was at eye level. Clat'Ha and VeerTa began to brief SonTag on progress at the mine. Qui-Gon heard their words, but he was distracted by something more important. There was a disturbance in the Force. He tuned into the disturbance, unsure of what it meant. The dark ripples were a warning, but of what?

The door suddenly flew open. A young man stood in the doorway. His shiny black cape was lined in a blue so deep it was almost black as well. A broken circle scar marked his cheek.

Qui-Gon's gaze locked with the intruder's. The moment hung suspended in the air. Then, to Qui-Gon's surprise, Xanatos broke into a delighted grin.

"Old friend! So you are here. I hardly dared to hope." Xanatos strode forward, handsome and commanding. His black hair flowed to his shoulders, and his dark blue eyes matched the lining on his cape. He gave the Meerian sign of greeting to SonTag, then bowed.

"Governor, I must apologize for my lateness. My transport was held up in an ion storm. Nothing was more important to me than getting here on time. I am Xanatos, the representative of Offworld."

SonTag greeted him, palms up. "I see that you already know Qui-Gon."

"Yes, I have that good fortune. But I haven't seen him in many years." Xanatos turned to Qui-Gon. He bowed.

There was no mockery in the bow, Qui-Gon noted. Just respect. Yet he did not trust it.

"I got your message on my arrival," he said neutrally.

"Yes, I had heard you were dispatched from Coruscant," Xanatos answered. "Since I had just been appointed Offworld representative, I knew we would meet. Nothing gave me more satisfaction."

Qui-Gon studied the young man. Sincerity rang in every word. What was going on?

"I see you mistrust me," Xanatos said. His midnight-blue eyes beamed a keen look at Qui-Gon. "Your sense of caution hasn't changed. But surely other Jedi apprentices have left the path of the Jedi without your mistrust?"

"Every apprentice is free to leave at any time. You know that," Qui-Gon said evenly. "If they leave honorably, there is no mistrust."

"And so I left. It was best for me, and for the Jedi," Xanatos said quietly. "I failed to lead that life. Yet it isn't a source of regret. I was not meant to live the life of a Jedi." Suddenly, he flashed a smile at SonTag, Clat'Ha, and VeerTa. "I value my training as a Jedi, but it didn't prepare me for the shock of reentry. I must confess that I went astray for a few years. That's the last time that Qui-Gon knew me."

Astray? Qui-Gon wondered. Is that how Xanatos thought of that time?

"But I've changed. Offworld has given me that chance."

Xanatos leaned forward, his gaze on VeerTa. "That's why I admire you, VeerTa. Offworld sent me to tell you that the company will not interfere with your project. A richer, more secure Bandomeer is better for all of us." Xanatos touched his chest. "I admire your leadership, because I love my home planet, too. Telos is always in my heart."

He turned to SonTag. "Perhaps if Offworld donated ten percent of its profits to the Bandomeer reclamation effort, it would convince you of our sincerity?"

SonTag looked flustered. Qui-Gon knew that even ten percent of Offworld's profits was an enormous sum. Offworld had never given away any profits to a charitable cause.

The offer must be a trick. Qui-Gon didn't trust it. But he could see that Xanatos had reached

SonTag and VeerTa. Only Clat'Ha still looked wary. But then, she had more reason to doubt Offworld. She had tangled with them recently.

Xanatos seemed to pick up on Clat'Ha's mistrust. He turned his penetrating blue gaze on her. "When I took my position with Offworld, it was with the understanding that certain policies would change. I do not believe in plundering planets and leaving them behind when we have gotten everything out that we want. Our actions on Bandomeer will be the first demonstration of our new policy."

SonTag nodded. "It's a wise course. And Bandomeer will be grateful for your help —"

Suddenly, a huge explosion rocked the room. VeerTa was knocked to the floor. Before the others could react, Qui-Gon was on his feet, lightsaber in hand.

Qui-Gon sensed the explosion had occurred outside the palace. He hurried to the window. VeerTa struggled to her feet and followed him.

At first, a large black cloud completely enveloped the view of the city below. Then the wind picked up, clearing the view.

A plume of smoke rose from a mineyard. Qui-Gon could see the rubble of a large building. One mine tower was down, and the other leaned dangerously. As they watched, it slowly tipped and fell, demolishing a shabby building, probably worker housing. Qui-Gon saw figures stumbling, running away from the disaster. There would be others trapped inside, he knew.

The sirens began, high-pitched and wailing. Beside him, VeerTa swayed, then gripped the sill to keep herself upright. "It's the Home Planet Mine," she whispered.

CHAPTER 5

*"I didn't start it," Xanatos would say when-
ever a fight broke out between him and another apprentice. His blue eyes would blaze
with sincerity and sorrow.*

*Like a father, Qui-Gon would always try
to believe him.*

VeerTa's hands curled into fists. She let out a
choked roar and threw herself at Xanatos.

Without seeming to move, Qui-Gon was suddenly between the two of them, holding VeerTa
off. It would do no good to attack Xanatos. Qui-
Gon knew firsthand how fierce and volatile a
fighter he was.

VeerTa struggled against Qui-Gon's iron grip.
"You did this!" she spat at Xanatos. "You'll pay
for it!"

Clat'Ha moved to stand beside VeerTa. Out-
wardly she was calmer, but her eyes betrayed

the same rage. "Of course they did it," she said contemptuously. "It's just their style. Cowards!"

Xanatos looked pale. "I assure you, Offworld had nothing to do with this. I'm confident that the facts will prove this —"

"Enough of your lies!" VeerTa shouted. She tried to spring at him again.

"Let us be calm," SonTag said urgently. "VeerTa, we must get to the mine. They'll need help."

"Yes, the miners —" VeerTa said. She rushed out.

Qui-Gon had seen the effects of explosions before. They were always terrible. Lives were lost, bodies maimed, spirits broken. Blood mixed with ashes and tears. He did not know why this tragedy seemed worse to him. Perhaps because the miners had carved the mine out of rock and earth. They had worked with no money and little hope to build a future they had struggled to even imagine.

They stacked the bodies in the yard. Qui-Gon worked tirelessly to carry victims from the wreckage. Forty miners were trapped below ground. Rescuing them was a painstaking and dangerous process.

The explosion had been touched off in one of the tunnels. The main administration building was completely destroyed, as well as the dwellings surrounding the mine. It was dark before Qui-Gon and the others had finished evacuating the wounded to med centers.

At last, there was nothing more for them to do. Clat'Ha called him to one of the untouched buildings for food and rest. He joined VeerTa and Clat'Ha at the table, but they were too exhausted and sorrowful to touch the food.

"Our dream has died," VeerTa said. Her face was filthy with dirt and mud.

"No," Clat'Ha responded softly. "That's what they want. We can rebuild."

The door opened, and SonTag entered. She, too, had helped at the mine today. Her red and gold tunic was filthy and caked with blood.

"We have news of the cause," she announced quietly. "It wasn't Offworld. There was a mixture of gases in a sub-level tunnel."

VeerTa half-rose. "Impossible!" she cried. "We have sensors —"

"The sensor was inoperative," SonTag said. "Strictly a mechanical failure. The engineers are certain of it."

Clat'Ha and VeerTa stared at SonTag in disbelief. "So it's our fault?" VeerTa asked numbly.

"I'm afraid it appears that way," SonTag replied. "Could someone have sabotaged the sensor?"

VeerTa shook her head. "We have the mine under twenty-four-hour guard."

SonTag spread her hands. "Mechanical failure is one of the hazards of mining."

Qui-Gon wasn't so sure. Something wasn't right here.

Just then, a knock came at the door. A miner handed a message to SonTag. She read it, then crumpled it in her hand.

"Bad news?" Clat'Ha asked.

"No, just surprising," SonTag said slowly. "Xanatos has offered the resources of Offworld to help rebuild the mine. Money, droids, anything we want. Plus, he'll house any displaced workers in Offworld housing."

"So he was sincere," VeerTa said, surprised.

Qui-Gon felt disturbed at this news. If this was a trap, it was a costly, elaborate one. Were the stakes so high for Xanatos? Surely he wouldn't go to all this trouble just to get revenge on Qui-Gon.

The site of the meeting had been moved at the last minute. The main building had been completely destroyed. If SonTag hadn't changed her mind, they would all be dead.

Xanatos was playing a game. Qui-Gon only wished he knew what the goal of the game was.

He was sure of just one thing: when it came to Xanatos, games had no rules.

CHAPTER 6

Obi-Wan was bored. If he had to go on one more Spore Tour, he would scream.

He knew that Agri-Corps did important work. But why was he here?

In the middle of brown, parched earth, the Agri-Corps had constructed a giant dome. Surrounding the dome were scientific laboratories and worker housing. Entrances from the labs and the admin centers led into the dome itself. Everyone worked for the good of the planet. No outside interests were allowed to control the research, and no profits were taken from any discoveries.

Obi-Wan would have found the operation interesting if it weren't for the fact that his tour guide, a Meerian named RonTha, was the dullest creature he'd ever met. RonTha was fascinated by such things as stem grafts and seed sprouts. He could talk about them for hours in his droning monotone. And he did.

The only bright spot was that Obi-Wan was about to be reunited with his friend Si Treemba, the Arconan he'd met on the transport.

Arconans were born in nests and raised in close communities. They didn't have a highly developed sense of individual self, and didn't often associate with outsiders. But Si Treemba had formed a deep bond of friendship with Obi-Wan. He had stood side by side with him against Hutts and Togorian pirates. Because of his decision to take Obi-Wan's side against the Hutt Offworld leaders, he had almost lost his life. Si Treemba had discovered his own individual courage along the way.

Obi-Wan headed for the admin center, where he was to meet RonTha and Si Treemba. He saw his friend waiting and hurried to greet him.

"It is good to see you again, my good friend," he said, clasping both of Si Treemba's arms. The Arconan had a strong, snakelike body with slender arms and legs.

"We are blessed to see you, Obi-Wan," Si Treemba answered. His large, glowing eyes were full of pleasure. Arconans rarely, if ever, used the word "I."

Clat'Ha had sent Si Treemba to monitor the Agri-Corps' dactyl research. The Arconans needed the yellow crystal to survive, and Agri-Corps was trying to develop a way to incorporate it into the food supply. It was unusual for one of his species to travel alone, but Si Treemba had become an unusual Arconan. Clat'Ha knew she could depend on him.

RonTha approached, consulting a datapad as he walked. "Today we are scheduled to tour the northernmost quadrant of the great dome," he told them in his usual drone. "We have many fascinating seed experiments to cover. Stay with me at all times, and do not touch anything."

RonTha led the way into the dome. The vast, enclosed space was lit by an artificial sun, actually an illumination bank set high in the dome. Outside the dome was a vast brown wasteland, but here they were surrounded by rustling grain and grasses. Around them gardeners hurried to and fro, their arms filled with flats of baby plants or seed dishes.

Dazzled by the light and heat, Obi-Wan and Si Treemba trailed after RonTha as he listed the many agricultural experiments taking place.

"With all this talk about food, we're getting hungry," Si Treemba whispered to Obi-Wan.

"We sure are," Obi-Wan agreed. He swallowed as he glimpsed a grove of trees ahead. Large, golden fruit hung from the many branches, close enough to pick.

A tiny monitor on RonTha's belt began to

glow. He switched it off. "I'm being called to the administration building," he told them. "You're free to wander about, if you wish. Just don't go off the path. And don't touch anything!" Ron-Tha hurried off.

Obi-Wan eyed the fruit. "Do you think when he said don't touch anything, he meant fruit?" he asked Si Treemba.

Si Treemba's triangular head bobbed nervously. "Hard to say."

"Probably not." Obi-Wan looked around, then quickly swiped a yellow fruit. He tossed it to Si Treemba, then got one for himself.

"We really shouldn't," Si Treemba said, biting into the fruit.

"Mmmffff." Obi-Wan waved a hand dismissively, chewing.

The fruit was sweet and succulent, yet had a crisp tang. It was the most delicious fruit Obi-Wan had ever tasted. "We'd better find someplace private to eat these," he said.

Just then, he and Si Treemba heard footsteps. They exchanged guilty glances, their mouths full. With a jerk of his head, Obi-Wan indicated that they fall back behind the trees.

A group of gardeners came into sight, carrying baskets. They headed for the orchard.

"Uh-oh," Obi-Wan whispered. "We'd better get out of here." He didn't want his mission to end with a disciplinary problem. He'd already had enough troubles on the journey here from Coruscant.

"Hey!" one of the gardeners yelled. "You there!"

Si Treemba began to choke and dropped the fruit. He tripped over it as he tried to run. Obi-Wan hauled him up and they dashed through the orchard, finally reaching a field. Obi-Wan yanked Si Treemba under cover of the tall grain.

"We'll have to cut through the field to get back to the main path," Obi-Wan panted.

They ran down the rows, trying to find a way out. The field was much larger than they'd thought. All they could see was green, and the artificial blue sky above.

Finally, they burst out of the last row. Obi-Wan felt his feet suddenly slide in something damp and marshy. They flew out from under him and he went flying. Si Treemba followed. Clots of dirt splattered their faces and tunics. They finally landed and slid into a huge pile of dirt.

"What's that smell?" Si Treemba said, wiping a clot of dirt out of his eye. "It smells worse than a bantha on a hot day."

"I think we found the fertilizer," Obi-Wan groaned, pulling himself out of the muck. They surveyed their surroundings. Behind them was the field. Ahead was a blank wall.

Something about the wall bothered Obi-Wan. It was tall and seamless, and curved out of sight around the fertilizer pile.

He walked closer and placed his hands against the wall. The surface was cool, like metal. When he took his hands away, to his surprise he saw, just for an instant, that his touch had caused a transparency. It happened in the flicker of an eyelid, too quickly for him to see inside.

"What are you doing?" Si Treemba asked impatiently. He let out the Arconan hissing sound of anxiety. "Let's go. This smell will kill us."

Si Treemba hadn't seen the wall flicker. Perhaps the Force was at work. "One moment," Obi-Wan said. "I think this might be another way out."

He felt carefully along the wall, watching as his fingers left a shimmering transparency behind. He'd never seen a metal with this quality before. Finally, he found what he was looking for — a seam. He traced it with a finger. It was a door.

Keeping his hands flat on the door, Obi-Wan felt the energy from the living things around him, the grain and fruit, the people, the rich, organic island that was the dome.

Si Treemba gasped when the entire wall suddenly turned transparent. They saw that it was actually an annex that extended back to the dome wall. Inside, Obi-Wan could see bags of fertilizer and cargo boxes of various sizes.

"It's just a storage area," Si Treemba said, disappointed.

It seemed innocent. So why had it been so well concealed? Obi-Wan pushed skillfully on the door. He heard a soft electronic beep, and it swung open.

Si Treemba hissed nervously again. His pale, luminous eyes flickered. "Are you sure we should go inside?"

"You stay here," Obi-Wan instructed. "Keep a lookout. I'll be right back."

He stepped inside the space. Immediately, the walls turned opaque again. It was like being inside a white cube. He bent over to examine the labels on the cargo boxes. The labels were black triangular shapes that showed a red planet with an orbiting holographic spaceship.

Obi-Wan recognized it instantly — Offworld. He leaned over to read markings on the side of the crate. He moved from box to box, reading the descriptive labels. Explosives. Turbo-drills. Detonators. Tunnel borers. Biotic grenades.

These were mining supplies. But they were on protected Agri-Corps land. Agri-Corps was strictly forbidden to concern itself with any profit-making enterprise. Was someone here secretly in league with Offworld?

"Obi-Wan, hurry up!" Si Treemba called. "We stink! We want to take a shower!"

Obi-Wan saw a small box in the corner that he had missed. This one had no label, only a metallic icon that served as a clasp. It was a broken circle.

He had seen enough for now. Obi-Wan slipped past the boxes to the door.

"What is it?" Si Treemba asked.

"Some kind of secret annex for Offworld," Obi-Wan said. "They're up to something."

Si Treemba's greenish skin paled to a dull gray. "Here? But they're forbidden."

"Since when does that stop them?" Obi-Wan said grimly. "Let's get back. I have to contact Qui-Gon."

"You mean you're not going to do anything?" Obi-Wan demanded. Qui-Gon wavered in front of him in miniature hologram form.

"There is nothing to do," Qui-Gon said. "Did you say the wall turned transparent with the Force?"

"I've never seen anything like it," Obi-Wan answered. "Have you?"

Qui-Gon ignored the question. "The information is interesting, nothing more. There's no real proof that Offworld is interfering with Agri-Corps research."

Obi-Wan wanted to howl in frustration. "They shouldn't be here at all! I should return to Bandor. Offworld is planning something . . . something big. We need to investigate this!"

"There is no need," Qui-Gon said crisply. "Your mission is to report back on the progress of Agri-Corps."

"What about the broken circle on the box?" Obi-Wan asked urgently.

"Obi-Wan, follow your orders," Qui-Gon sternly replied. "If you find proof of wrongdoing, contact me immediately. Do not take any action on your own."

"Qui-Gon —"

"Did you hear me, Obi-Wan?"

"Yes," Obi-Wan answered reluctantly.

"Now, I must go. Keep me informed."

The hologram wavered, then disappeared. Obi-Wan stared at the empty air where Qui-Gon's image had hovered. Once again, Qui-Gon had shut him out.

CHAPTER 7

There was a time when the circle was not broken. There was a time when everything was as it seemed. When there were no se-crets.

The broken circle. Had Obi-Wan mistaken it? Or was Xanatos involved in Agri-Corps?

He couldn't tell the boy. Obi-Wan would demand answers that Qui-Gon wasn't willing to give. It was better to keep the past in the past.

Besides, the boy must learn patience.

Qui-Gon headed for the Home Planet Mine. It was amazing how much work had been done since the explosion. The mine was scheduled to go back into operation in only a week. Offworld had followed through on its promise, and had given money and droids. They had already cleared away debris from the tunnels, and were working on shoring them up again.

Clat'Ha waved at him from across the yard. She was heading into the mine with her workers. She'd barely stopped to sleep or eat since the explosion.

Qui-Gon opened the door to the temporary office, a hastily erected metal shed. VeerTa sat at a monitor that recorded the details of the operation. When she spun around in her chair, he saw that her face was alight with excitement.

"There is good news," VeerTa said in a low tone that throbbed with excitement. "The explosion has done us a great service, Qui-Gon. It blasted deeper into the ground than we've ever gone before. We've discovered a vein of ionite."

Qui-Gon was impressed. Ionite was one of the most valuable minerals in the galaxy.

"Do you know what this means? No one has ever found ionite on Bandomeer. Traces, yes. But our main resource is azurite." VeerTa leaned forward, her gaze intense. "The Home Planet Mine will be the only source. The profits are potentially enormous. This can save the entire planet!"

"It is good news," Qui-Gon agreed cautiously. It was one thing to find a valuable mineral. It was another to keep control of who mined it.

"You already see the problems ahead," VeerTa said shrewdly. "Then we must keep this a secret. I haven't even told the members of the board. Only Clat'Ha knows. If Offworld discovers this, they will easily drive us out of business and grab the vein for themselves. The explosion blew up all the azurite we've already mined. Technically, we're bankrupt."

"What's your plan?" Qui-Gon asked.

"Thanks to Offworld, we have money," VeerTa said. "True, they gave it in order to buy our trust by helping us rebuild. But we can use it to mine the ionite. We just need a few weeks to get everything operational. Then Offworld can't stop us."

VeerTa's face blazed with determination. Qui-Gon allowed himself to feel her enthusiasm. But at the same time, he wondered why VeerTa was letting him in on the secret. He waited, knowing there was more.

"Let me show you what we found," VeerTa said, rising.

He followed her into the mine. She gave him the protective headgear and led him into the south lift tube. "The K region is safe," she assured him. "We've managed to shore up Core 6. We know through sensing devices that the new vein is below it. It's a level we haven't even dug to yet."

K-7. Core 6. Startled, Qui-Gon looked at the instrument panel on the elevator. As they descended, the indicator lights clicked on. *Core 10. Core 9. Core 8. Core 7 . . .*

The nightmare rose in Qui-Gon's mind with all its dark power. "Is there a Core 5?" he asked VeerTa.

She shook her head. "We don't have the technology to go that deep. It's too close to the planet core. Offworld has developed deeper core technology, but if we try to buy or lease it, we could tip them off. We hope to get enough ionite out of Core 6." The Core 6 light glowed, and the elevator stopped.

Qui-Gon exited the tube and started to turn left.

"No," VeerTa said. "The tunnel is completely blocked that way."

She hit a switch near the door, and lights set into the rock walls glowed. Qui-Gon could see now that the tunnel was narrow and low-ceilinged, with a hydraulic track that ran down the center. The tunnel curved to his left and was swallowed up by inky blackness. There was a pale, bluish cast to the light glistening off the blue-black rock, reflecting the presence of azurite.

"Clat'Ha and I came to see the damage," VeerTa went on. "The lift tube in the north tunnel was damaged, but it should be operational in a few days. We have to fix that first."

She turned right and led the way down the tunnel. A pile of rocks lay in their path, and a hole had been blasted in the tunnel floor. "The blast must have reacted with some gases below this level," she explained. "Here, the blast moved upward." She bent down and picked up a rock. She scratched it with a fingernail. Qui-Gon caught the glint of a dull silver glow. "Clat'Ha noticed this. We took it back to study. She had a hunch, and she was right. Ionite. We dropped sensors and saw how much we had."

"You're going to have to be careful," Qui-Gon said. "If Xanatos finds out —"

VeerTa nodded. "That's why we need you. We'd like you to join the board of directors of Home Planet. With you on the board, Offworld wouldn't dare try to undermine us. They'd have to go up against a Jedi."

Qui-Gon was already shaking his head. "Jedi are forbidden to take part in any profit-making enterprise," he said. "We can't profit from our protection. It's an unbreakable rule."

"But think of the riches you'd be entitled to!" VeerTa said urgently. "You wouldn't have to keep them for yourself. You could donate them."

"I'm sorry, VeerTa," Qui-Gon said firmly. "I'll help in any way I can. But this I cannot do."

VeerTa looked disappointed. Obviously, she

didn't understand the role of a Jedi. "I'll have to be satisfied with that, then," she said. Her eyes glittered as her gaze roamed the mine shaft. "It's all here. Our future. I only pray we will succeed."

"I will do everything in my power to ensure it," Qui-Gon promised. Something told him the task would not be easy.

CHAPTER 8

Obi-Wan told Si Treemba about his conversation with Qui-Gon. The Arconan nodded, as if he'd expected it.

"Clat'Ha would say the same," he said. "We need more proof."

"Just what I was thinking," Obi-Wan declared.

Si Treemba hummed with nerves. "The last time you had that look in your eye, we ended up in a Hutt prison."

"Relax," Obi-Wan said. "We're only going to stake out the annex tonight. We'll go for a little stroll in the dome, then wind up there. What can go wrong?"

"Any number of things," Si Treemba moaned.

Obi-Wan and Si Treemba stretched out flat between two rows at the edge of the field. They pulled a green tarp over their heads for warmth and camouflage.

"You might as well go to sleep," Obi-Wan said. "I'll take the first shift."

"If you're sure," Si Treemba mumbled. He closed his eyes. A moment later, he began making the snuffling sound Arconans make when they sleep.

Obi-Wan had felt charged with excitement about the stakeout. After only an hour, however, his eyelids began to droop as well. He couldn't fall asleep! Maybe he could take a quick exploratory tour. That would wake him up.

He slithered out of the field and stood. Brushing himself off, he headed for the door to the annex. He wanted another look at that sealed box with the broken circle on it. Something told him that Qui-Gon had recognized the mark. Maybe there was a way to ease it open without anyone knowing he'd tampered with it.

Once again, he used the Force to open the door. Everything was exactly where he had left it. He crossed to the box.

Just as he reached it, he heard a noise behind him. He whirled around and saw a hooded figure approaching. At first he thought it was Si Treemba, wrapped in the tarp. Then he realized it was a stranger in a shiny black cape.

"Who are you?" he asked. He felt the uneasy ripple of something dark in the Force.

"A friend," the hooded figure said. "Someone who was once just like you." He threw off the hood. His blue gaze was warm and friendly. "I used to be his apprentice, too."

"Qui-Gon's?" Obi-Wan asked suspiciously. "I'm not really his Padawan. And everyone says his Padawan died."

"Is that what they say?" the man asked. "Yet here I am. What else do they say?"

"That Qui-Gon's Padawan disgraced the Jedi," Obi-Wan said. "And betrayed Qui-Gon."

The man's eyes burned blue fire. "Is that Qui-Gon's story?" Then the hard lines of his face relaxed. "I was his Padawan. So I know what you go through every day, Obi-Wan Kenobi. I know what you wait for. His approval. His trust. But he keeps both from you. He keeps a skin of ice around himself. The more you try to please him, the farther away he goes."

Obi-Wan said nothing. The words seemed to have come from his own heart. At his worst moments, it was exactly what he thought.

Xanatos looked compassionately at the boy. "Yoda praises him. The Galactic Senate depends on him. Everyone vies to be his apprentice. But he is the worst kind of Master. He

denies you his trust. Yet he demands everything of you."

Obi-Wan heard the words as if he were in a
trance. *How true it is*, he thought. Deep anger
stirred, anger that lay dormant inside him. He
feared his anger more than any enemy.

"I am Xanatos," the man said. "Did he ever
mention me to you?"

Obi-Wan shook his head.

Xanatos gave a sad, rueful smile. "No," he
said softly. "He would not. It's up to me to tell
you what he did to me. How he built me up,
kept me by his side, always with the promise
that I would advance. Yet in the end, he broke
every promise. It will happen to you, too, Obi-
Wan."

Could it be true? Could Qui-Gon's coolness
hide the seeds of betrayal? Obi-Wan had felt the
chill of Qui-Gon's reserve, but he always assumed it was because Qui-Gon hadn't accepted
him. Did Qui-Gon's secrecy hide evil, or good?

"Why are you telling me this?" Obi-Wan
asked warily.

"To warn you," Xanatos said. "That's why I
came. You —" He stopped suddenly. He held up
a hand. "Someone is coming," he whispered.

Suddenly, five security officers burst in. Obi-
Wan saw the red planet patch on their uni-

forms. Offworld! What was their security force doing in the dome?

One of the men spoke into a comlink. "We found the thieves," he said.

"No," Obi-Wan said. "We're just —"

But Xanatos had drawn his lightsaber. Obi-Wan watched in surprise as Xanatos charged. Only Jedi carried such weapons. The guards drew their blasters, and Obi-Wan had no choice. In the blink of an eye, he had powered up his own lightsaber and joined the battle.

He felt the reassuring weight in his hand as he wielded the weapon, knocking a blaster from a guard's grasp. He knew Qui-Gon would not want him to kill Offworld guards. It could make a bad situation worse back in Bandor.

So he fought defensively, while Xanatos became the aggressor, spinning through the air to deliver scorching hits. But he, too, seemed reluctant to land a killing blow.

Xanatos's Jedi skills must have been rusty. He allowed himself to be maneuvered into a corner. The guards advanced with blasters drawn. Obi-Wan leaped on top of a pile of crates and threw himself into the group, arms and legs scissoring the air. Two guards went down firing, and he felt searing pain in his shoulder. Still, he was able to kick the third guard's blaster from his hand.

The guard suddenly produced an electro-jabber. He raised it against Xanatos as Obi-Wan raced to stop him.

Obi-Wan deflected the move with his lightsaber, but the electro-jabber dealt a glancing blow against his ribs. Blinding pain shot through his body. He reached out for the Force dizzily, but someone smashed him from behind. His vision turned gray and fuzzy, and he sank to his knees.

The last thing he remembered was hitting the floor.

CHAPTER 9

Now Qui-Gon could see his mistakes. He had been blind to Xanatos' faults. He indulged the boy. He gave without seeing. He was a failure as a Master, because he trusted the apprentice too much. He let his fondness blind him to what he should have seen all along.

After some reflection, Qui-Gon decided to ask SonTag and VeerTa if they had seen a box like the one Obi-Wan had described. They had both visited the Agri-Corps Enrichment Zones many times. Perhaps there was a simple explanation for what Obi-Wan had found.

Qui-Gon described the box, and VeerTa nodded. "I've seen a box like that."

"So have I," SonTag agreed, thinking. "In the Western Enrichment Zone. I was just there recently."

"I think I saw one at the Northern Zone," VeerTa added. "It was with other equipment. I'm sure it contains Agri-Corps instruments."

It was exactly the response Qui-Gon had been hoping for. The box must not be significant. In the other zones, it had been in plain view.

So why was he worried?

Maybe because it had been placed with Offworld mining equipment. Obi-Wan couldn't have been wrong about that.

Back in his quarters, he jacked into his data pad to investigate Offworld. He was curious about what position Xanatos held. His former apprentice had been uncharacteristically silent on that subject. If he was a high official, wouldn't he have boasted of his title?

Qui-Gon searched Offworld company records. He could find no mention of the name Xanatos. Which meant what? Either Xanatos had been lying about his involvement, or his position was a secret within his own company. But why?

Qui-Gon clicked a few more keys. The head of the company was anonymous, but a board of directors was listed. Qui-Gon recognized most of the names, rulers of worlds that were virtually controlled by Offworld. Figureheads.

There were no answers . . . yet. But he had an idea where to look for them.

It was time to pay a visit to Offworld Head-quarters.

Offworld did not try to beautify their Bandomeer office. The building, a black, windowless block, echoed the grim mines that surrounded it.

Qui-Gon entered the center hall with its azurite-studded walls. The mineral was its only decoration. A Hutt security guard sat behind a black cube that served as a desk. His body rolled past the confines of the desk. He turned flat, dead eyes toward Qui-Gon.

"I have come to see Xanatos," Qui-Gon said.

"Move, wretch," the Hutt replied, bored. "Take your petty complaints to your immediate supervisor. There's no one here anyway. Xanatos is on an exploration trip to the northern mine quadrant." The Hutt reached for a blaster. So much for corporate hospitality.

Qui-Gon didn't move a muscle. He concentrated on the Hutt's greasy mind, pulling in energy from the Force.

"Perhaps I should wait in his private office," he said.

"You should wait in his private office," the Hutt repeated tonelessly. "Take the restricted lift tube to Horizon Thirty."

"Security controls should be lifted," Qui-Gon said.

"All security controls shall be lifted."

Qui-Gon entered the tube marked RESTRICTED. There was only one indicator light, for Horizon Thirty. The lift tube reached the floor in seconds. He stepped off into a reception area. The chairs were made of stone. The cubelike desk was empty. He could see no door to another room, just a blank, empty wall.

A blank wall . . .

He placed a hand against the wall. When he took it away, he saw a brief flicker of transparency.

Obi-Wan's description tugged at Qui-Gon's memory. He'd read about the technological advances on Telos, the home planet of Xanatos. Recently they had been able to cover transparisteel with a special coating that rendered it opaque. When a thermoelectrical impulse was generated, the wall returned to normal transparency.

He pressed his whole body against the wall and it turned transparent. He could see the inner office. Still, where was the door?

Qui-Gon drew the Force in and felt it move within him like a cresting wave. The entire wall became transparent. Then the hidden door swung open. As soon as he was inside, the wall was once more opaque.

It was a clever system, Qui-Gon thought, walking toward the enormous stone desk. Xanatos could control the transparency from the reception area. He would be able to see inside the office before he entered. If someone managed to slip past security checks, the intruder would be unable to hide in the office.

How like Xanatos. Concealing and revealing. He'd forgotten how clever his apprentice was about secrets. He would reveal something, leading you to think he had told you everything. But what he revealed was always a trifle. He kept his most important secrets under his control.

The only piece of furniture in the office was the stone desk. Qui-Gon pressed a button, and a data pad rose from the top of it. He accessed the filing system. Just as he suspected, it was holographic.

The files rose before him. He flipped through the directory. He wasn't sure what he was looking for. There was a file on the Home Planet Mine, and he accessed it. It wasn't very helpful, just a list of money and droids that had been loaned after the explosion. He closed it.

Then he saw a file directory with no name. An icon hovered where the label should have been. Two broken golden circles that overlapped. Qui-Gon's heart beat faster. The two broken circles could be read as letters, too. O and C.

Offworld Corporation.

Qui-Gon accessed the directory, but a warning red light pulsed.

"Password, please," a voice said.

Qui-Gon hesitated. Knowing Xanatos, he had only one chance to get it right. And if he didn't, Xanatos had surely rigged the hologram to alert him that someone had tried to break in.

It was a risk. But he had to take it.

"Crion," he said, using Xanatos' father's name.

The directory flipped open. He scanned the list of files. To his dismay, they were all written in code. He would never have time to break it. And if he removed a file, Xanatos would know he'd been there.

But he'd gotten what he'd come for, anyway. Qui-Gon closed the filing system thoughtfully. Two broken circles had formed the initials of Offworld Corporation. Perhaps others would see that as a coincidence. But he knew that nothing was casual to Xanatos. Qui-Gon's instinct told him that he had found the person who controlled Offworld. Perhaps Xanatos had even founded it. But why would he keep it secret? *So he could maneuver more easily*, Qui-Gon guessed. Xanatos had always preferred stealth and trickery to achieve his ends. The question was: what was Xanatos after?

CHAPTER 10

Qui-Gon was sure Xanatos was ready. He had spent years with the boy, watching him become a man. His mastery of the light-saber was unsurpassed in his class. His ability to focus on the Force matched his Master's. He passed the preliminary tests with a near-perfect score. Qui-Gon was ready to welcome him as a Jedi Knight. It was a proud moment.

But Yoda was not so sure. Yoda said there would be one last test.

The holographic picture of Yoda rose before Qui-Gon. The transmission was clear. His heavy-lidded eyes blinked slowly, making him appear bored, but his long ears twitched. Qui-Gon had come to recognize the sign of the Master registering surprise.

"So Xanatos could be planning a great evil,

you say," Yoda said. "That you have discovered this is good, Qui-Gon. Yet time to react, it is not."

"But I suspect he might be planning to take over Bandomeer," Qui-Gon protested. "This planet has no resources to fight. It must be prevented before it happens."

"But safety is your concern, is it not? Demand that you move slowly, that does. Proof of a plan you do not have," Yoda pointed out. "Read the files, you could not."

"I can read *him*. Xanatos."

"Ah, so certain, are you? Certain you always were about him."

Qui-Gon fell silent. In his quiet way, the Master had rebuked him. Yes, he had been certain about Xanatos. He had defended him against every gentle warning Yoda had given.

"You have pushed aside your past for too long, Qui-Gon," Yoda said, after a pause. "Running from it, you are. Yet you can run a little longer before you turn and fight."

"If you say, Master." Qui-Gon tried to hide his impatience. He struggled to consider Yoda's wisdom. It was never wise to dismiss his advice.

"Use Xanatos' tactics against him, you must," Yoda offered. "He plays with you. Play along for now, you will. Give him room to make a mistake. Slip he will. The trick is to wait for it."

"Yes," Qui-Gon said. "I see a path now." He began to sign off, but Yoda held up his hand.

"One last thing I have," he said. "A question, it is. Why do you leave Obi-Wan in the dark, Qui-Gon? He knows not of this, I think. Yet he is on the same trail you are on, in a different place."

"That's true," Qui-Gon admitted. "But there is no need for him to know yet. It places him at risk. I'm keeping him out of danger."

"The apprentice accepts the danger when the Master accepts the apprentice," Yoda replied.

"You forget," Qui-Gon said coolly. "I did not accept Obi-Wan. He is not my apprentice. We are on a planet together. There is a difference."

Yoda nodded slowly. "Trust is the difference. Easier you think, to change the past than the future."

Qui-Gon felt irritated. "That's illogical," he said. "You can't change the past."

"Not logical, yes," Yoda agreed. "Then why do you think it?" Still nodding, Yoda ended the communication.

Qui-Gon stood at the window, looking east over Bandor. As usual, Yoda had made him question himself. Why had he rebuffed Obi-Wan's efforts to help? And what if he'd placed the boy in more danger by not warning him about Xanatos?

He had been wrong. Although it sometimes took him too long to come to that conclusion, once he did, he acted swiftly.

He activated his comlink and sent a message to Obi-Wan. Usually, the boy answered immediately. After ten minutes had passed, Obi-Wan grew worried. He sent a message to Si Treemba. No answer. He closed his eyes, gathering the Force. He felt it then, something dark, a void. Obi-Wan was in danger.

Someone pounded on his door. He crossed to it, already knowing it would be bad news.

Clat'Ha stood in the hallway. Her sleek red hair was awry, and her green eyes were full of worry.

"Si Treemba just contacted me with news," she said. "Obi-Wan has disappeared."

CHAPTER 11

With his eyes closed, he heard the sound of the sea. Or was it the pounding in his temples?

Cautiously, Obi-Wan opened his eyes. He was in a long, narrow room with a low ceiling. Rows and rows of sleeping platforms surrounded him. Bedding was rolled up at the foot of each wide platform. He was alone. His lightsaber was gone, as was his comlink.

His ribs and shoulder were bandaged. Something was around his neck. Obi-Wan ran his fingers around it. It was a collar. It felt smooth, with no obvious clasp to remove it. It hummed underneath his fingertips. Maybe it was some sort of healing device.

When he raised his head, a sharp pain made him release his breath in a hiss. Obi-Wan breathed slowly, calming his mind as he'd been taught. He accepted the pain. He welcomed it as a friend, advising him that his body had been injured. He thanked it for alerting him to this. And he focused his will on healing.

After only a moment or two, the pain lessened slightly, enough for him to stand. There was a narrow window high above him. He balanced on a sleeping platform and stood on tiptoe to see out of it.

Despair filled him. A great, gray sea stretched before him for kilometers. There was no sign of land. No ships. Only this huge platform, with tall towers rising from the sea.

He knew where he was at once — the Great Sea of Bandomeer, which covered half the planet. He must be on some sort of deepsea mining platform. The deepsea mines were only whispered about. They were rough, dangerous places that many miners did not survive.

"So you're awake."

Obi-Wan turned, startled. A tall, mournful creature stood in the doorway. His skin was dark, but appeared to be peeling in white patches. Two white circles surrounded his eyes. He had extraordinarily long, rubbery arms that dangled past his knees.

"How are you feeling? I was worried," he asked, but before Obi-Wan could respond, he chuckled. "I lie! Not so!"

"Who are you?" Obi-Wan asked. He felt dizzy,

and he commanded his mind to clear. He stepped down carefully from the platform.

"The name is Guerra, not that you need to know it so. I'm a Phindian. We're a mixed lot, here. Which reminds me, Human boy. Move."

Guerra's arm shot out suddenly. It reached across two sleeping platforms and fastened on Obi-Wan's wrist. "I don't have all day. The guards will be here with electro-jabbers for both of us if I don't get you outfitted."

"Outfitted for what?"

"Outfitted for what? A vacation on a Syngia moon!" Guerra chortled. "Not so, I lie! Mining, of course."

"But I'm not a miner," Obi-Wan protested as Guerra dragged him toward the doorway.

"Oh, so sorry. In that case, you don't have to work." Guerra's odd, patchy face leered at him. "Instead, you can be thrown off the platform. You'll have such a lovely swim —"

"Not so?" Obi-Wan guessed.

Guerra chortled and slapped Obi-Wan on the back, sending him flying. "Good one, Human boy! Not so! Thrown off to drown. Except the fall will kill you first! Now, come along."

Guerra pushed him through the doorway. A cold wind hit his face. Around him were piles of mining equipment. Droids were busy hauling beamdrills to a lift tube, where workers were waiting. Guards were everywhere on the platform, patrolling with electro-jabbers and blasters.

As they climbed stairs to the second level, Obi-Wan saw that the platform was much bigger than he'd thought, about the size of a small city. Hydrocrafts sped back and forth from the deepsea platforms that ringed the main structure.

Guerra pushed him into a storage room. He rubbed his eyes to survey the equipment, and the white patches around his eyes widened. Obi-Wan realized that Guerra's skin was actually fair. He was covered with mining dust and grime.

Guerra caught him staring. "Showers once a month, but why bother? Soon, you'll look like me, Human boy."

"Guerra, I'm not a miner," Obi-Wan repeated. "I've been kidnapped and sent here. I'm —"

Guerra burst out laughing. He slapped his knees with his flapping hands. "Kidnapped? How awful! Let me alert the security forces! Oh, I lie again! How do you think I got here? Do you think I volunteered? We're all slaves, don't you see? At the end of five years, they give you enough pay to transport off-planet and start over. If you survive. Most don't."

"Five years?" Obi-Wan asked, swallowing hard.

"That's the contract you sign," Guerra said. "You'll need a thermosuit. And a tech-helmet. Some tools . . ."

"But I didn't sign a contract!"

Guerra laughed again as he held a thermosuit against Obi-Wan and rejected it as too small. "Stop distracting me with jokes, Human boy! Did I sign? They forge it so!"

"My name is Obi-Wan Kenobi. I am a Jedi pupil."

"Jedi, Kedi, Ledi, Medi," Guerra said in a nonsense singsong. "Doesn't matter who you are. You could be the Prince of Coruscant. No one will find you here." He tossed another thermosuit at Obi-Wan. "This one will have to do. So, now for a tech-helmet."

Obi-Wan clutched the suit against him. It was stained and damp. He couldn't imagine putting it on. He was already chilled to the bone. His head pounded again, and he touched it carefully. He could feel the bruise on the back of his scalp. Blood matted his hair. His ribs were on fire.

Then he remembered the collar. He touched it. "Is this some sort of healing device, Guerra?"

This time, Guerra fell back into the pile of

thermosuits. He laughed so hard he began to choke. "So! You make me laugh again, Obawan. Healing device!" He hooted with laughter, then cleared his throat. "Not so! It is an electro-collar. If you try to leave the mining platform, ga-coosh!" Guerra's rubbery arms waved. "You blow up!"

Obi-Wan touched the collar gingerly. "The guards can blow us up?"

"Not the guards," Guerra explained cheer-fully. "Electro-collars are activated on the main-land. Just in case of a rebellion, you see. If we overpowered the guards, we might be able to dismantle the devices, got it? So the guards can't blow us up, no." Guerra smiled amiably at him. "They can only beat us and blast us and stun us and throw us overboard."

"What a relief," Obi-Wan muttered.

Guerra grinned, his teeth flashing yellow. "I like you, Obawan. So! I'll watch out for you — ha! Not so, I lie again! I trust nobody and no-body trusts me. Now hurry before the guards come and give us a stun." Guerra poked him and made a sizzling sound, then laughed up-roariously. "Don't look so sad, Obawan. Tomor-row, you'll probably be dead!"

Obi-Wan climbed reluctantly into the thermo-suit. He grabbed the tech-helmet and strapped on the servo-tool belt. He had no choice. Not yet. He had to figure out how to escape. Guerra said that no one had ever done it. But a Jedi had never been here before. He hoped.

Obi-Wan cleared his mind. He pushed away his fear and despair. He focused on the collar around his neck. Surely he could use the Force to override the device.

He concentrated hard, bringing the Force around him to bear on the collar. He used every ounce of his training and discipline.

But the collar still hummed with its electro-charge.

He was too weak, perhaps. He would have to bide his time.

If he survived . . .

As he returned to the deck, he saw a guard viciously stun a miner who had stumbled. How *could* he survive this?

Play along for now, you will.

The words came to him clearly. Yoda's words. Just hearing the tones of the Jedi Master pushed the despair away and gave him courage.

Obi-Wan lifted his head. He was a Jedi. He would play along. And he would survive.

CHAPTER 12

"We have one last mission," was all Yoda would allow Qui-Gon to say to Xanatos. "And then you will become a Jedi Knight. . . ."

Si Treemba knew nothing. Clat'Ha told Qui-Gon that one minute Si Treemba had been asleep and the next, he woke to find Offworld guards hustling Obi-Wan away. Obi-Wan had been unconscious. Qui-Gon's heart twisted at this news.

Si Treemba had not seen anyone resembling Xanatos. Still, Qui-Gon knew he had to be involved. He had been away from Bandor. Surely that was no coincidence. He'd heard from Son-Tag that Xanatos had since returned.

Yoda had told him not to confront Xanatos directly. But that was before he knew that Obi-

Wan had been kidnapped. The rules of the game had changed.

Of course, he should contact Yoda with an update and await instructions from the Council. But he wouldn't. He was tired of being played with. This wasn't just a game. Xanatos was taunting him, daring him to risk open confrontation, and now he had involved the boy.

As an apprentice, Xanatos' chief failing had been overconfidence. Qui-Gon hoped it still was.

Qui-Gon knew that Xanatos was overseeing the operation of Offworld's largest azurite mine on the outskirts of Bandor. He waited until dusk.

He watched Xanatos leave the small, cramped administration building that served the mine and the adjoining smelting plant. The shifts had just changed, and the area was clear of miners. All the administrative workers had left. Just as Qui-Gon had hoped.

Slag piles rose around the yard. Offworld never bothered to keep the mining area clean of debris. The sky was dark gray fading to black. Yet the lights had not been turned on in the yard, probably to save money. Anyone arriving late for a shift would have to feel their way to the mine.

Qui-Gon waited until Xanatos had crossed the yard. Then he moved from the shadows of the slag pile into Xanatos' path.

Xanatos stopped. There was no surprise on his face. He wouldn't allow himself to show it, not even in a deserted yard at near dark when his oldest enemy appeared out of nowhere.

Qui-Gon expected no less. "If you have plans for Bandomeer, you should know I am here to stop you," he said.

Xanatos flung one side of his cloak behind him. His hand rested casually on the hilt of a lightsaber. Xanatos had broken a solemn rule by leaving the Jedi and retaining it.

Xanatos patted the lightsaber. "Yes, I still have it. After all, I trained for all those years. Why should I give it up like a thief, when I deserve to carry it?"

"Because you deserve it no longer," Qui-Gon answered. "You shame it."

A flush spread over Xanatos' face. Qui-Gon's comment had hit its mark. Then he relaxed, smiling. "I see you are still a hard man, Qui-Gon. Once that bothered me. Now it amuses me."

Xanatos began to circle around him. "We were friends at the end, more than Master and apprentice."

"Yes," Qui-Gon said, tracking him, moving with him. "We were."

"All the more reason for you to betray me. To you, friendship is nothing. You enjoyed my suffering."

"The betrayal was yours. As was the enjoyment of suffering. That is what you discovered on Telos. Yoda had already seen it. And that is why he knew you would fail."

"Yoda!" Xanatos spat out the word. "That knee-high troll! He thinks he has power. He hasn't dreamed of a tenth of the power I know!"

"*You* know?" Qui-Gon asked mildly. "How do you know such power, Xanatos? A mid-level manager of a corporation, sent to do the board's bidding?"

"I do no one's bidding but my own."

"Is that why you're here? Is Bandomeer a test of your abilities?"

"I don't take tests," Xanatos snapped. "I make the rules. Bandomeer is mine. All I have to do is reach out my hand and take it."

He circled closer, his cloak swirling and brushing against Qui-Gon. "It's a tiny planet. Galactically insignificant. Yet it pours forth wealth into my hands. If you would only lose the tiresome rules of the Jedi, it would do the same for you. But no, Qui-Gon is too good. He is not tempted. He is *never* tempted."

"Bandomeer is not yours to own." Qui-Gon pulled an arm's length away from Xanatos.

"You were always overconfident. You have gone too far this time."

"No." Xanatos' dark blue eyes glittered. He drew his lightsaber. "*Now* I have gone too far."

In a flash, Qui-Gon's lightsaber hummed to life. When Xanatos leaped to deliver his first blow, Qui-Gon was already moving to deflect it. Their sabers met and sizzled. Qui-Gon felt the power of Xanatos' stroke move up his arm.

Xanatos had not lost his fighting edge. He had only grown more powerful, moving with economy and grace. His lightsaber flashed, he *thrust* and *thrust* again, always with a surprising twist or direction.

Qui-Gon moved defensively. He knew he would not be able to tire Xanatos, one method of Jedi strategy.

Xanatos had more than physical skill. Qui-Gon could feel the power of his mind. Xanatos was still in touch with the Force. He had gathered the energy of darkness, not light.

Qui-Gon leaped aside to avoid another blow. Xanatos laughed. It was time to change the rules of engagement. Enough defense.

Qui-Gon sprang at Xanatos, his lightsaber humming and flashing. He delivered one blow after another, which Xanatos deflected. Smoke and sizzle filled the air. Xanatos laughed again.

Qui-Gon used a slashing sequence of moves to position Xanatos against the wall of the building. But Xanatos leaped onto the slag heap and flipped over in midair, landing on Qui-Gon's other side.

"You destroyed everything I loved," Xanatos accused, his lightsaber barely missing Qui-Gon's shoulder, so close it singed the fabric of his tunic. "You destroyed me that day, Qui-Gon. Yet I was reborn. Stronger, wiser. I have surpassed you."

Their lightsabers tangled, buzzing furiously. Qui-Gon felt the charge in his arm, but didn't waver. Xanatos kicked out with a foot, but Qui-Gon was expecting it, and moved aside. Xanatos lost his balance. He almost fell, but recovered in time.

"Your footwork has always been your weakness," Qui-Gon said dryly as he dealt a blow to Xanatos' shoulder. Xanatos twisted away, but not before Qui-Gon saw him grimace with pain. "If you've surpassed me, it is only in your mind."

Perhaps it was the taunt. Perhaps it was because Qui-Gon had finally caused him real pain. Xanatos whirled the other side of his cape behind his shoulder. A second lightsaber was suddenly in his hand.

Startled, Qui-Gon lost his focus for an instant. There was only one person to whom that lightsaber could belong.

"And where is your new apprentice?" Xanatos sneered.

So Xanatos had been responsible for Obi-Wan's disappearance. Now he knew it for sure.

Xanatos faked a charge to the left, went right, then danced back to the left again. Qui-Gon remembered the move from the Temple. He easily blocked the blow.

He was fighting the past. His past. Perhaps he could defeat Xanatos, but the battle would not be won. Only the future mattered now. Obi-Wan was the future. The past would wait.

Qui-Gon paused, knowing Xanatos was ready to escalate the fight. Ready to deliver a death blow, if he could.

Suddenly, Xanatos whirled around, took three long steps up the slag heap, and pushed himself off, flying through the air with both lightsabers slashing toward Qui-Gon, every muscle ready to drive the blows home.

He met empty air. Qui-Gon twisted away, grabbing Obi-Wan's lightsaber from Xanatos' unprepared grip.

Then, for the first time in his life, Qui-Gon ran from a battle. He had to find Obi-Wan. The cold wind whistled past his ears as he crossed the mine yard at top speed.

He heard Xanatos' voice rise from the mist.

"Run, coward! But you can't escape me!"

"It appears that I have!" Qui-Gon shouted.

Xanatos' laugh was chilling. "Only for now, Qui-Gon. Only for now."

CHAPTER 13

For two nights and two days, Obi-Wan struggled to use the Force to override his electro-collar. His wounds were healing slowly. His body was worn down by work in the mines.

The miners were kept in half-starved condition, but if anyone faltered, the guards beat them savagely with an electro-jabber. All of the guards were Imbats, creatures known for their size and cruelty, not their intelligence. They were as tall as trees, with leathery skin and massive legs ending in broad, grasping toes. Their heads were small for their bodies and dominated by large, drooping ears.

Lift tubes took the miners below the sea floor. The small tunnels were hazardous. There were frequent leaks, and occasionally a tunnel would burst, drowning everyone inside. But what the miners dreaded most was a backflow of bad air into the tunnels. It was a slower death by suffocation.

"I've been looking forward to today," Guerra remarked as they waited for their turn on the lift tube.

Obi-Wan's heart dropped. Whenever Guerra was especially pleased, he knew he was in for trouble. Guerra dealt with the terrors of mining by treating it as a huge joke played on them all.

"Why?" he asked warily.

"You there!" a guard shouted. Obi-Wan stiffened, but the guard crossed to a Meerian who had stopped to adjust his servo-tool belt.

"Stop holding up the line!" he bellowed, lashing out with the jabber. The miner cried out and crumpled to the floor. The guard kicked him aside. "No food for three days for that!"

Nobody tried to help the Meerian. They all knew that they would get the same treatment. Obi-Wan squeezed into the tube with Guerra.

"Today we go to the deepest sublevel," Guerra said. "Traces of ionite."

"What's wrong with ionite?" Obi-Wan asked.

"Even traces of the mineral carry an alternate charge," Guerra explained. "Not positive, not negative, void. So! The instruments can go dead. If bad air backflow happens, no warning. Makes the work fun. Ha! Not so." His yellow eyes stared bleakly at Obi-Wan amid the white circles.

"Last week Bier's warning timer went dead because of the high ionite concentration," another miner said. "He was in an aquasuit, out mapping the sea floor. Ran out of oxygen and didn't make it back to the tunnel."

Obi-Wan watched the indicator lights tick down their descent. He felt like a void himself. He had absolutely disappeared. He was deep under the sea floor, in a place where Qui-Gon would never think to look.

And even if Qui-Gon could trace him . . . would he actually save him? Xanatos' mocking words sang in Obi-Wan's mind. Would Qui-Gon betray Obi-Wan as Xanatos claimed he had betrayed his former apprentice? Would Qui-Gon leave him to die?

Obi-Wan thought that nothing could be worse than the grinding hard work during the day. But at night, the guards loosened their controls. The miners needed some sort of outlet. Fighting was their amusement of choice. They had nothing to lose, and bets were placed according to a complicated system of how badly someone would be maimed. The night before, a miner had lost an eye. Obi-Wan learned to stay out of the way.

He left the miners' quarters and found Guerra out on deck. It was bitterly cold, but Guerra didn't seem to feel it. He lay stretched out on the metal deck, watching the stars.

"Someday I'll get back up there," he told Obi-Wan.

Obi-Wan sat on the deck next to him. "I'm sure you'll make it, Guerra," he said.

"So! I'm sure, too," Guerra said. Then he murmured "Not so," softly under his breath.

"Guerra, you've been all over the rig. Have you ever seen a box with a broken circle on it?" Obi-Wan asked.

"So, sure," Guerra answered to Obi-Wan's surprise. "I just had inventory detail. They rotate the job so no one gets a chance to steal. There was a box like that in the explosives room. It wasn't listed on my sheet, but the guards told me to shut up about it. So I did. I'm not stupid!"

"Do you think you could get me into the explosives room?"

Guerra bounced up. "I hope that's a joke, Obawan. You get thrown off the platform for stealing!"

"I'm not going to steal anything," Obi-Wan promised. "I just want to look."

Guerra smiled. "Great idea, Obawan! Let's

go!" He lay down again. "Not so, I lie. I stick out my neck for nobody, remember?"

"What if I knew a way to dismantle your electro-collar? We could steal a boat and make it back to the mainland."

Guerra gave him a sidelong look. "If this is true, why does your collar hum, my friend?"

"I can do it," Obi-Wan said. "I'm waiting for the right moment." He knew that as soon as he recovered completely from his injuries, he would be able to harness the Force. He had to. "Trust me."

"I trust no one," Guerra said softly. "Ever. That's why after three years I am still alive."

"Well, what do you have to lose?" Obi-Wan asked urgently. "Just bring me to the guard, then show me where you saw the box. I'll take all the blame if I get caught."

Guerra shook his head. "The guard will never give up the keys. It's against regulations."

"Just leave that to me," Obi-Wan said.

"I need to do some extra checking," Guerra told the guard. "I need the keys."

The guard raised his electro-jabber. "Get lost or you're over the side!"

Obi-Wan summoned the Force. He knew he didn't have the power to alter physical objects.

But he was counting on the fact that the small, limited mind of an Imbat would bend to his will.

"That might not be a bad idea," Obi-Wan said. "We should check the supplies again."

"Might not be a bad idea," the guard said, tossing Guerra the electronic keys. "Check the supplies again."

Guerra stared at Obi-Wan. "What did you do, Obawan?"

"Never mind," Obi-Wan said. "Hurry."

Guerra led him to the explosives' room. He opened the door and Obi-Wan hurried inside.

"Where's the box?" he asked. "Guerra? Just show me and then you can go."

Guerra paused in the doorway. His yellow eyes went wide. "I hear footsteps," he whispered. "They're running. It's the guards! Must be a silent alarm on the door."

"Come in and close the door!" Obi-Wan hissed.

But instead, Guerra began to shout. "He's in here! I found him!" He turned to Obi-Wan sadly. "Even though I'm in danger, I would never betray a friend. So —"

"Not so," Obi-Wan finished for him as the guards rushed in.

Guerra pointed, and the guard brought his electro-jabber down on Obi-Wan. Pain sent him crashing to his knees. He felt himself being carried to the lockup and thrown in.

"Penalty for stealing is being thrown overboard," he heard a guard say.

"My shift is over," the other one replied with a yawn. "Tomorrow morning is soon enough."

CHAPTER 14

The trip to Telos should have been uneventful. Yoda had found someone willing to transport them, a pilot ferrying a shipment of droids to the Telos system. From the first, tension sparked between the pilot and Xanatos. Stieg Wa was young, brash, and confident. He'd been on his own since he was a child and had prospered in treacherous adventures. He good-naturedly needled Xanatos about being sheltered in the Jedi Temple and knowing nothing of real life.

Perhaps Yoda had foreseen the clash of personalities. Perhaps this was another test. Qui-Gon warned Xanatos to keep his temper, to not let the pilot's genial barbs affect him. Smiling, Xanatos assured Qui-Gon that he would.

The one danger of the journey was crossing the Landor star system, known to be overrun with pirates. Stieg Wa was confident that they could slip through; he'd done it countless times. But when three pirate ships ringed the transport and warned Stieg Wa to surrender, he discovered that a crucial indicator light was faulty. The transport's cloaking system had malfunctioned.

Stieg Wa, refusing to surrender, pushed the small transport, evading blaster fire in a stunning display of skill. After they lost the ships, Stieg Wa announced that the cloaking system had been sabotaged. He blamed Xanatos. Qui-Gon, of course, believed Xanatos when he swore he had nothing to do with it. Why would he risk pirates attacking a ship he was on?

Stieg Wa was out on the dorsal platform fixing the device when the pirates returned. He was hit by blaster fire and captured.

Xanatos led Qui-Gon to the escape pod. He had already programmed the coordinates for Telos. When Qui-Gon asked him why he'd taken such a precaution, he smiled.

"I always make sure I have a back door," he said.

Dawn was still an hour away when Qui-Gon strode off the transport toward the Enrichment

Dome. The Meerian sent to meet him hurried forward. "I am RonTha. I'm happy to welcome —"

"Where is Si Treemba?" Qui-Gon interrupted crisply, striding toward the main building.

"H-he is in the dome, waiting for you," RonTha said, running to catch up to Qui-Gon's long stride. "But protocol must be followed. You must register with —"

"Show me to him," Qui-Gon demanded.

"But protocol —"

Qui-Gon fixed his gaze on RonTha. He didn't need to use the Force. The Meerian crumpled under the force of his irritation.

"This way," he said, scurrying forward.

A rustle of grain announced Si Treemba's presence. He sprang out of the field when he saw Qui-Gon.

"We've been watching since Obi-Wan was kidnapped," he said. "No one has been in or out."

Qui-Gon looked compassionately at Si Treemba. The young Arconan looked so tired Qui-Gon wouldn't have been surprised if he fell asleep on his feet.

"We shouldn't have fallen asleep that night," Si Treemba said. "Obi-Wan said he'd take the first watch. We should have stayed awake. . . ."

"Now is not the time to rethink the past," Qui-

Gon said gently. "We only have the now. We must find Obi-Wan. What did you see?"

"Not much," Si Treemba admitted. "A group of men in Offworld uniforms carried him away. We followed them, but we lost them in the dome." Si Treemba hung his head.

Qui-Gon tried not to show his frustration. Si Treemba felt bad enough as it was. But how could he find Obi-Wan on such scant information?

Suddenly, Qui-Gon noticed that RonTha looked very nervous. The Meerian was perspiring and looking about as if he wanted to escape.

Qui-Gon turned his full attention on him. "Did you see anything, RonTha?"

"Me? But we're forbidden to be in the dome at night," RonTha protested. "Against all protocol."

"You didn't answer my question," Qui-Gon said politely.

"I try to follow the rules," RonTha said.

"And do you always succeed?" Qui-Gon asked kindly. He tamped down his impatience. "Anyone can be tempted to break rules."

"The fruit is so good," RonTha whispered. "Just a snack before bed . . ."

"Tell us," Qui-Gon said firmly.

RonTha swallowed. "I was in the orchard when I saw them. A group of men carrying something. Someone led them. Someone in a black cloak . . ."

Qui-Gon nodded encouragingly.

"At first I just hid. But then I saw that they were carrying Obi-Wan. He was under my charge! I was responsible for him. So I followed them to the sea landing."

Qui-Gon frowned. "They left by sea?"

He nodded. "Two of the men, with Obi-Wan."

Where could they be going? Qui-Gon wondered. The sea was vast, and there were no islands or reefs. "Did they say anything?" he asked.

"Nothing of significance," RonTha said. "Something curious, though. One of them said to Obi-Wan that he would see him in five years, if he survived. Obi-Wan didn't answer, of course. He was still unconscious."

"Five years?" Qui-Gon repeated.

"The deepsea mines!" Si Treemba exclaimed.

Of course, Qui-Gon thought. Where better to hide Obi-Wan than on a deepsea mining platform?

"Find me an Agri-Corps boat," Qui-Gon ordered RonTha.

"But it is against proto —" RonTha's voice faltered under the impact of Qui-Gon's icy glare. "Yes, immediately," he agreed.

Qui-Gon pushed the motor of the hydrocraft as high as it would go. He rocketed across the gray sea just inches above the waves. RonTha had been able to give him the precise coordinates of the mining platform, and he'd entered it into the boat's onboard computer. Besides, RonTha assured him, the platform would be too big to miss.

It began as a darker gray smudge on the gray horizon line of the sea. As Qui-Gon drew closer, the smudge formed into towers and buildings, a small city in the middle of the sea.

Qui-Gon focused a pair of electrobinoculars on the platform. He scanned it for any sign of Obi-Wan. Suddenly, he saw movement on the very edge. A group of men were pushing something . . .

Qui-Gon's grip tightened as he zoomed in on the sight. It was Obi-Wan! Guards were jabbing him with the dull ends of electro-jabbers, pushing him toward the edge of the platform. They were going to push him off!

Qui-Gon gunned the motor. It was already at top speed. In despair, he realized that he was too far away. His only hope was that Obi-Wan would survive the fall, and he'd be able to pick him up.

He raced across the flat sea, closer and closer.

Obi-Wan was at the very edge. Qui-Gon's heart contracted with pain. To lose him this way! He would never forgive himself.

But as he raced toward Obi-Wan, a movement caught his eye from a lower level of the platform. Someone had fashioned a kind of sling out of a spun carbon tarp. He was tying it on the struts that supported the main platform. As Qui-Gon watched, two long, flexible arms shot out, positioning the sling in midair.

Obi-Wan fell. Qui-Gon watched the fall through the electobinoculars. Obi-Wan's face was grim but composed, free of terror. Determined to fight to the last, but accepting death if it came.

Like a Jedi.

Then Obi-Wan saw the sling below. Across the distance, Qui-Gon felt ripples of the Force originating in Obi-Wan. He focused his own will to meet it, concentrating the Force, willing Obi-Wan's body to twist toward the tarp.

Obi-Wan seemed to grab on to thin air and pull himself to the left, shifting in mid-fall. He bounced onto the middle of the sling. In another second, those long arms shot out and pulled Obi-Wan to safety.

Qui-Gon was almost to the platform now. He heard the furious cries of the guards as they saw what had happened. They turned away, racing toward the lift tube to the lower floor.

Qui-Gon pulled up, bobbing in the sea as he quickly threw a carbon-rope over one of the struts and tied the craft securely. Then he threw another rope onto the platform where Obi-Wan had disappeared. He tested it, then climbed up.

Obi-Wan was racing down the hallway with the long-armed creature. Suddenly, he stopped, as if Qui-Gon had called his name, though he'd said nothing. Obi-Wan turned to see Qui-Gon leap over the railing.

"I hoped you would come," he said.

Qui-Gon nodded. "Almost too late. Hurry."

"This is Guerra," Obi-Wan said, pointing to his rescuer.

"Bring him. The guards are coming," Qui-Gon said urgently. "They saw what happened."

Guerra's hands flew to his collar. "I can't leave. Neither can you, Obawan."

Obi-Wan looked at Qui-Gon. "It's an electro-collar. It will blow us up if we leave."

Qui-Gon nodded. He concentrated the Force on Obi-Wan first. He sent neutral energy to the transmitter.

Obi-Wan touched the collar. "The buzzing is gone."

"We'll have to find a way to remove it on the mainland," Qui-Gon said.

"That's where the transmission signal is," Guerra explained. "The guards in the security office on the Bandor loading dock carry the transmitter."

Qui-Gon brought the Force to bear on Guerra's collar but wheeled suddenly. Behind him, the lift tube opened. Blaster fire zinged past his ear.

"You'll be needing this," he said to Obi-Wan and tossed him his lightsaber.

Two lightsabers hummed in unison as they turned to face the guards. The four Imbats hesitated. They had never seen such weapons. But, still infuriated at Obi-Wan's escape, they rushed forward.

Qui-Gon leaped onto the railing, somersaulted in the air, and landed behind them. Obi-Wan charged from the front. They moved in a graceful duet, advancing, retreating, forcing the guards back toward the lift tube and deflecting blaster fire with ease.

"More guards coming, Obawan!" Guerra yelled.

Fifteen guards shot out of the stairwell at the far end of the platform, firing as they ran.

"Time to go," Qui-Gon told Obi-Wan.

With a cry, Guerra crumpled, hit by blaster fire. He looked up at Obi-Wan. "Just a graze," he said. "Go. I'll hold them off for you."

Obi-Wan pressed a blaster in his hand. "No, you go. Up the stairwell. And hide. In an hour, your collar will be deactivated for good. Trust me."

Guerra smiled weakly. "I . . . trust . . . no one," he said softly. But as Obi-Wan and Qui-Gon deflected blaster fire, he managed to limp to the stairs. Guerra turned. "Not so, Obawan! I trust you."

Obi-Wan vaulted over the fallen guards, climbed onto the rail, and jumped toward the rope. He slid down and landed in the hydro-craft.

Qui-Gon followed. He gunned the motor. With blaster fire raining over their heads, they made for the open sea.

CHAPTER 15

As soon as they were out of reach of blaster fire, Qui-Gon set a course for Bandor. Obi-Wan sat at his side, looking ahead. He did not know what to ask first.

"You said you *hoped* I would come," Qui-Gon remarked quietly. "Not *knew,* but *hoped.*"

Obi-Wan didn't speak for a moment. "I need to know about Xanatos," he said finally. "He told me you betrayed him. That he was your apprentice, and he trusted you."

"Did you believe him?" Qui-Gon asked.

Obi-Wan paused. The wind blew his hair back from his face. "I don't think you would betray a Padawan," he said at last. "But I don't understand why he hates you so. Does he have cause, Qui-Gon? Did Xanatos arrange to have me imprisoned on the mining platform just to get back at you?"

The Jedi Master nodded grimly. "Yes, I believe so. It's time I told you about him. I should have told you before."

Mist had begun to rise on the sea. Obi-Wan could taste the droplets on his lips. Gray surrounded him in a whirling circle, silver-gray mist above, dull gray sea below. Qui-Gon's words seemed to come at Obi-Wan from a past as misty as the surroundings, as far away.

"Each Jedi apprentice brings something unique to the Temple," Qui-Gon began. "Even at a young age, Xanatos stood out. His intelligence was fierce and quick and agile. He was a leader. I thought he was the most promising boy to the come to the Temple in many years. So did Yoda."

Qui-Gon paused. He made a small correction to the steering of the boat. "Yet Yoda had questions. As Xanatos grew and I took him as my apprentice, I resented Yoda's hesitations. I thought Yoda was questioning my judgment. Of course, he was questioning the boy. He saw something that I did not. When Yoda suggested one last mission, I was glad. At last, I thought, I can prove to Yoda that I was right. Xanatos will prove himself, prove what I'd seen all along."

Qui-Gon turned to Obi-Wan. "You see my failing here." It wasn't a question.

Obi-Wan nodded. "I think so. What *you* could prove. What *you* wanted."

"So it was a test for me, too," Qui-Gon said. "I didn't know that at the time. I let my ego and pride take over. My need to be right. It's important that you know this, Obi-Wan. Even a Jedi Knight is still a living being, with the same failings."

"We are not saints, but seekers," Obi-Wan said, repeating a Jedi saying.

"Yoda sent us to Telos, the home planet of Xanatos. Xanatos had not seen his father Crion in many years. In that time, Crion had grown in power. Telos is noted for its scientific research. Telosian scientists are brilliant innovators. Crion used their discoveries to create great wealth for the planet. And for himself. He built on his power and ruled the planet as governor. Yet he did not rely on advisors or his Senate. He ruled alone. Xanatos saw how powerful his father was. How luxurious a life he led. All of the riches of the galaxies were at Crion's fingertips. Xanatos saw this, and a hunger began to grow in him. An anger. He saw that in taking him away, we had deprived him of a different kind of power. *I* had deprived him. He hated the Jedi for that."

Qui-Gon stared out into the mist. "We give up many things when we choose this life, Obi-Wan. We are destined to have no home, no measurable power. Xanatos had these things in his grasp. Crion saw his son weaken. He had come to regret his decision to let Xanatos go. He was an old man and had driven away every friend, every ally. So Crion urged Xanatos to join him in his great plans. I saw that Yoda sensed this would happen, that this was the last, great test."

Qui-Gon sighed. "I did not doubt Yoda's wisdom. I did what I knew I should. I stepped back. I did not attempt to guide Xanatos. He was ready to make his own choice."

"He made the wrong one," Obi-Wan said softly.

"Crion had grown greedy, as the powerful often do. He had secret plans to wage war against a neighboring planet. It was not enough to have the research. If Telos had access to the resources — the minerals, the factories — it could grow even more powerful. The treaty between the two worlds was automatically extended every ten years. This year, Crion called for a renegotiation. I found out later that it was a ruse, a way to delay until he could raise an army. I was to monitor the negotiation. Xanatos deliberately sabotaged the first meeting, according to his father's direction. They wanted to enrage the population of Telos, you see. But I knew, and I revealed what I knew to the people of Telos. They rose up against Crion. But Crion did not retreat. Xanatos urged him to fight instead. They hired an army to put down the rebellion and stay in power. Civil war broke out. Suddenly, people were dying. The situation was out of my control. And all because I did not see clearly what Xanatos was capable of."

Qui-Gon gripped the controls of the boat. "Xanatos led the army. The last battle was fought at the governor's quarters. Crion was killed."

Qui-Gon paused, his expression grim. "I killed him," he said solemnly. "In front of his son I dealt the killing blow. My lightsaber sliced through the ring on Crion's finger. As he lay dying, Xanatos picked it up from the fire where it had fallen. He pressed the hot metal to his cheek. I can still hear the sound of the burn. You can still see the scar."

"A broken circle," Obi-Wan said.

Qui-Gon turned to face Obi-Wan. His face was bleak, harsh with memories. "He said the scar would serve to remind him always of what I had taken from him. How I had betrayed him. The fact that thousands had died bevause of his father's greed meant nothing to him. The weight of those deaths meant everything to me."

"What happened?" Obi-Wan asked.

"He drew his lightsaber against me," Qui-Gon said, his gaze shifting to once again take in the past. "We battled to the point of exhaustion. At last I knocked the lightsaber from his hand and stood over him. But I couldn't deliver the fatal blow. Xanatos laughed at me. He ran out. I searched Telos for him, but he had stolen a transport and the treasury and had escaped into deep space. He disappeared without a trace . . . until now."

CHAPTER 16

Qui-Gon looked at the instruments. "We're approaching Bandor harbor."

"We have to get the transmitter," Obi-Wan told Qui-Gon. "I promised Guerra."

Qui-Gon nodded and headed toward the Offworld loading dock. They tied the hydrocraft and headed for the Offworld security office.

"Do you have a plan?" Obi-Wan asked.

"We don't have time for a plan," Qui-Gon said, kicking open the door. Three Imbat guards looked up in surprise. Before they could make a move toward their blasters, Qui-Gon's lightsaber sang through the air. The three blasters clattered to the floor as the guards clutched their wrists and howled.

"Transmitters, please," Qui-Gon remarked pleasantly. When they hesitated, he casually brought his lightsaber down on the power terminal. It sizzled and collapsed into a molten heap.

The three guards exchanged frightened glances. Then they threw down their transmitters and dashed out the door.

"It's nice when it's easy," Qui-Gon remarked. He bent down and picked up the three transmitters. Striding back onto the dock, he threw two in the sea. Then he pressed the button on the third.

"Guerra is free," he said. "Now let's see if we can get that collar off."

Qui-Gon placed his large hands around the collar, searching for a catch or seam. He could not break the collar, or twist it apart. He set his lightsaber to lower power and tried to cut it, but could not.

"I need a high power, and that would injure you," he said.

"Or behead me," Obi-Wan pointed out cheerfully.

Qui-Gon smiled briefly. "We'll just have to find a way to get it off in Bandor." He tossed the transmitter to Obi-Wan. "You'd better keep this until it's off.

Obi-Wan tucked the transmitter into an interior pocket of his tunic. "What now?"

Qui-Gon's blue eyes gleamed. "Xanatos." He said the name like a curse. "We need to get back to Bandor."

Qui-Gon climbed into the driver's seat of an Offworld security landspeeder.

He powered up the vehicle, and Obi-Wan jumped in. The landspeeder roared toward the city in the distance.

The gray sky was dark and low. The mining towers in the distance looked like spidery traces against it, growing larger as they sped toward Bandor. As they reached the outskirts, Obi-Wan saw a dot on the horizon.

"Someone heading this way," he said.

Qui-Gon nodded. He had seen it. Obi-Wan felt something dark in the Force. He glanced at Qui-Gon.

"I feel it, too," Qui-Gon murmured.

Within minutes, a speeder bike was upon them. They didn't need to see the black cloak to know who was piloting it.

"Hang on," Qui-Gon said. "I don't think Xanatos is in the mood to chat."

"He's got laser cannons!" Obi-Wan shouted.

A blast from the cannon missed them by centimeters, sending up a shower of dirt and gravel.

"So I see," Qui-Gon said.

He wheeled the landspeeder sharply, turning to the right as another blast whistled past them.

Lightsabers were useless. They had no blasters. They had to rely on Qui-Gon's skill. Even as he drove, he gathered the Force around him, using it to anticipate the blasts.

Dirt and grit flew in their faces as Qui-Gon swerved, dived, reversed, and hung stationary, all to evade the deadly laser cannon. On a speeder bike, Xanatos had greater maneuverability, and he used it to dodge suddenly around them, firing from the left. The jolt nearly sent Obi-Wan flying out.

"Hang on!" Qui-Gon called. He sped ahead, as low to the ground as he dared. He kicked up the dust underneath him, which blew behind them in a thick cloud, blinding Xanatos.

It bought them precious seconds, no more. Qui-Gon recognized the mining towers ahead. It was the Home Planet Mine. There would be friends there, weapons. Clat'Ha was a fierce fighter. She had saved his life once before.

He roared into the yard, but no one was there. Everyone was in the mine, working to repair it. There was no time to call VeerTa or Clat'Ha. Behind them, they could hear Xanatos roaring into the yard.

Qui-Gon jumped out of the landspeeder, calling on Obi-Wan to do the same.

Xanatos headed for Qui-Gon and Obi-Wan at top speed. Qui-Gon unsheathed his lightsaber and dealt Xanatos a glancing blow as he sped past. But the impact sent Qui-Gon spinning backward, and he felt his shoulder wrench in pain. They could not fight Xanatos while he was on that vehicle.

Xanatos turned and roared back toward them. They had no choice but to dash into the mine entrance. As they did, Qui-Gon had a sudden flash of chilling knowledge.

They were doing exactly what Xanatos had planned for them to do. They were playing his game.

Qui-Gon drew Obi-Wan back into the tunnel. It branched off in several directions, and he tried to remember which way VeerTa had led him to the lift tube. He let the Force direct him, take him over. He ran down the left tunnel, Obi-Wan at his heels. The lift tube stood at the end of the tunnel. They jumped in and Qui-Gon pressed the number of the deepest level, Core 6.

The glow lights hummed as they stepped out into the tunnel. Qui-Gon turned to the left.

"Where are we going?" Obi-Wan asked in a whisper.

"There's another lift tube," Qui-Gon explained. "It should be fixed by now. Xanatos wouldn't know that. We'll be able to circle around him to come at him from another direction, or even escape the mine. It's better not to fight here."

Obi-Wan nodded. It was always best to fight

in a place where your opponent couldn't drive you into a corner.

But that wasn't the only reason Qui-Gon wanted to escape the mine. Xanatos had driven them in here for a purpose. They needed to foil that plan. A nameless dread tugged at Qui-Gon, telling him there was something here he would not want to face.

They traveled deeper into the tunnel. Qui-Gon frowned as he peered ahead. "VeerTa said this tunnel was completely blocked. Why —"

Suddenly, a shadow detached from the wall of the tunnel. Xanatos stood before him.

"You make so many mistakes, Qui-Gon," he said. "It's a wonder you're still standing. First, you deactivate the transmitter so that I know exactly where you are. Then you enter the mine, which is exactly what I wanted you to do. And then you assume that I don't know about the north lift tube."

Behind him, Qui-Gon heard the hum of Obi-Wan's lightsaber.

"Which one of you shall I kill first?" Xanatos murmured. "You, or your clumsy boy?"

Obi-Wan lunged forward fiercely. He leaped onto a mining cart, which rolled toward Xanatos. At the last moment, Obi-Wan sprang off. He flew over Xanatos' head, striking down with his lightsaber as he did so.

Qui-Gon heard the flesh on Xanatos' hand sizzle. Howling, Xanatos almost dropped his lightsaber, but caught it with his other hand.

Obi-Wan landed safely behind Xanatos. "Don't call me clumsy," he said.

Whirling so quickly Qui-Gon had barely caught the movement, Xanatos sprang at Obi-Wan. The boy leaped back, slashing with his lightsaber at the same time. Xanatos' attack missed him by a whisper. Qui-Gon was already charging forward, and Xanatos turned to parry the thrust. Their lightsabers tangled and locked, sputtering. Smoke rose in the tunnel.

Xanatos withdrew, leaping past Obi-Wan, and the two Jedi pursued him down the tunnel. As they ran, the floor beneath them sloped sharply. Qui-Gon realized that they were descending to a lower level.

Turning a corner, they just had time to see Xanatos disappear into a smaller corridor that led off the shaft. They hurried forward. The crosscut tunnel was narrow and dark. The glow lights here were set at a fainter setting. The ground dropped sharply downward. Xanatos was gone.

"Wait, Qui-Gon," Obi-Wan panted. "Are you certain we should follow?"

"Why not?" Qui-Gon asked impatiently. His lightsaber pulsed hot in his hand.

"Because he wants us to," Obi-Wan said simply.

"It's too late now," Qui-Gon said. "He has chosen the field of battle, true. But we can defeat him."

Qui-Gon turned and ran down the tunnel after Xanatos. Obi-Wan followed. He would stand by Qui-Gon's side until his very last breath.

They were deep in the planet's crust now, close to the core. The heat was intense. Qui-Gon saw a faint sign glowing ahead. *Core 5.*

VeerTa had lied to him. Or else she had not known this tunnel existed.

The tunnel opened out into a slightly wider one. The glow lights were brighter here. Immediately after they left the smaller tunnel, a hidden panel slid shut behind them.

They were trapped.

Qui-Gon and Obi-Wan slowly circled, their lightsabers held at the ready. There was no sign of Xanatos.

Then the lights went out.

The mocking voice came from out of the void. "I hope the two of you have time for a Temple exercise." Suddenly, in the darkness, the red glow of lightsaber extended.

Qui-Gon didn't wait for Xanatos to strike. He moved through the blackness toward the glow. He could not see, he let the Force guide him. He could feel his opponent, feel the dark tremors of his evil. He struck.

"Missed me," Xanatos said. "I was always best at the blindfold test. Remember?"

Obi-Wan moved off to the right, hoping that between them, he and Qui-Gon could catch Xanatos in a classic pincer movement. But suddenly the lightsaber was moving through the air, slashing toward him. He jumped back just in time. He smelled lightning in the air from the close call.

It was hard fighting now, driven by instinct and with only the Force to help them. Xanatos was a cunning, powerful adversary. He attacked and retreated in a furious rhythm, faster than any fighter Obi-Wan had met. Qui-Gon's grace and power were astounding as time and time again he met Xanatos with his thrusting lightsaber, protecting himself and Obi-Wan from blows.

Obi-Wan dived to the floor, hoping to slash at Xanatos' legs and get him down. But Xanatos sidestepped and somersaulted over him. He felt the brush of air as he went by.

Obi-Wan tried to push away his own anger and use the white light of the Force. His mind had been too clouded by anger. He needed to get clear. It was their only hope. He drew on the living Force to guide him.

Suddenly, he saw Qui-Gon take a step back. His lightsaber flickered for a moment. Had he felt Obi-Wan's shift?

Obi-Wan felt Qui-Gon's Force energy suddenly flow into his, melding and pulsing in a white heat. Qui-Gon's lightsaber glowed green again, so bright it illuminated the shaft. Together, they sliced through the air, never stopping, moving, sliding, swerving. Xanatos was driven back, back, until they had him cornered against a tunnel wall. But suddenly, the wall turned transparent, and a door opened. Xanatos sprang inside.

"It's a lift tube!" Qui-Gon cried, rushing forward. But the transparent door closed. Qui-Gon struck at it with his lightsaber, but the light only sputtered.

Xanatos' voice echoed through the cavern through some sort of amplification device. "It doesn't matter what you do now. The mine is about to blow. I've created the same conditions for explosion as I did last time. Except more so. Gases are mixing and will combust. I have enough time to get to the surface. You do not."

They heard the lift shoot up out of the mine.

The voice of Xanatos echoed in the darkness.

"Good-bye, my old Master. May your death be as painful as my father's."

CHAPTER 17

"The crosscut tunnel," Obi-Wan gasped.

Together, they ran back to the entrance. But, as they suspected, it was sealed. Qui-Gon put his hands against it. It was coated transparisteel. In the dimness, it would look like a wall. The entrance to the tunnel from the main shaft would be concealed that way, too.

"It's sealed," Qui-Gon said. "And I cannot open it. Not with the Force."

"Together then," Obi-Wan suggested. They concentrated, drawing the Force to bear on the door. It did not open, or even turn transparent.

"There is a stronger lock on this one, I think," Qui-Gon said. "Xanatos wouldn't risk our being able to open it."

"There has to be a way," Obi-Wan cried in frustration. He struck the door with his light-saber, but felt only a painful shock move through his arm.

"There's a panel here," Qui-Gon said. He opened it. Several buttons glowed. He pushed them, but nothing happened. "Some sort of locking device," he muttered.

"He said we didn't have much time," Obi-Wan said. He glanced around the tunnel. "Qui-Gon, he said the blast will be more powerful . . ."

"Yes," Qui-Gon answered. "And I'm sure he was sincere."

They exchanged a look. Both of them thought of the miners above, and Clat'Ha and VeerTa. Many lives would be lost. The dream of the Home Planet Mine would die. Bandomeer would be lost as well.

"There's only one thing to do," Obi-Wan said. "I can get us out of here. I'm the only one who can."

Qui-Gon felt deep unease stir within him. "What do you mean?"

Obi-Wan touched the electro-collar around his neck. "I have the transmitter," he said. "I can reactivate it. If I push myself up against the door, the explosion should open it. You might have time to evacuate the mine."

"But you'll never survive the blast!" Qui-Gon exclaimed.

Obi-Wan reached into his tunic for the transmitter. "Stand as far back as you can," he instructed Qui-Gon.

"No, Padawan. There has to be another way."

"There is no other way, and you know it," Obi-Wan said steadily. "Now stand back."

"No!" Qui-Gon cried. "I will not! And I order you not to do this."

"Qui-Gon, think of the many who will lose their lives," Obi-Wan said urgently. "Think of what Xanatos will win. Think of Bandomeer. Our mission was to protect it. If I don't do this, we fail."

"This is not the way," Qui-Gon said grimly.

Obi-Wan's face was white and still. Determination tightened every muscle. "Yes, Qui-Gon. I can do it. I *will* do it."

CHAPTER 18

Qui-Gon was back in the nightmare. He felt the same horror, the same despair. The same sense that he must prevent this thing, even as he admired the sheer courage of the boy who had suggested it.

"I won't allow it," he told Obi-Wan. "I'll use the Force to neutralize the collar."

Obi-Wan shook his head, a small smile on his face. "You won't be able to. I know I can fight you, and win. Maybe just this one time. But this time I'm right, and you are not."

Qui-Gon was taken aback. He felt the Force emit from Obi-Wan like a breaking wave. The power of it astonished him. He locked his gaze with Obi-Wan. Their wills clashed silently in the dark tunnel.

Obi-Wan pressed himself against the seal, holding the transmitter against himself. "Let me go, Qui-Gon," he said. "It is my time."

Desperately, Qui-Gon looked at the seal panel. He wanted to smash it with his lightsaber. Wanted to slam his body against the door. He could not let this happen!

He would not let the nightmare win.

The nightmare . . .

The broken circles glowed at him. Why hadn't he noticed them before? The Offworld secret logo was on the seal panel.

The circle that brings the past to the future, yet does not meet. He must make the circle meet. He must bring the past forward. He must . . .

"Wait." Qui-Gon quieted his mind, letting the Force fill him. He drew from Obi-Wan's power as well, concentrating on the broken circle. He envisioned the circle moving, meeting, becoming whole once more. The past would meet the future and create the present. That was what mattered. Xanatos was past. Obi-Wan was now.

Slowly, the separate strands moved, making a perfect circle.

The door slid open.

"I told you there was an easier way," he said to Obi-Wan.

Obi-Wan grinned in tired relief. Perspiration streaked his face from the heat and effort. "We'd better hurry."

They raced back up the tunnel, following the twists and curves to the main shaft. Qui-Gon remembered an emergency siren near the south lift tube. He activated it, and pulsating sound filled the mine tunnels.

"Evacuate," a voice said calmly. "Evacuate."

"That means us, too," Obi-Wan said, pressing the button for the lift tube.

But Qui-Gon hesitated. He glanced around the tunnel. They had been working down here to clear it. Boxes of explosives stood stacked against the walls. And one box rested on top.

"Obi-Wan," Qui-Gon said. "Is that the box you saw?"

Obi-Wan turned. "Yes," he said. "But there's no time to find out what's in it." The lift tube arrived with a whoosh. "Let's go, Qui-Gon!"

Qui-Gon didn't answer. He walked over to the box. He unsheathed his lightsaber and, with great precision, cut the lock.

"He always had more than one trick," he murmured. "He always had a back door." He lifted the lid carefully. Just as he'd thought. It was an ion bomb, the most destructive explosive in the galaxy.

Obi-Wan stood by his shoulder. "He said he had mixed gases."

"He lied," Qui-Gon said. "This bomb is on a timer. And my guess is that all those boxes stored around Bandomeer are set to blow at the same moment." He turned to Obi-Wan. "The chain reaction will be enormous. The entire planet could blow."

Obi-Wan went pale. "Do you know how to dismantle it?"

"The Force won't work," Qui-Gon said, crouching. "This is a trigger so delicate that the Force itself might set it off. I can do it, but I need time. More time than I have." Qui-Gon bent closer. "This appears to be the master control. Xanatos must have set it when he left. That's the good news. If we can disarm this one, none of the other bombs will blow."

Obi-Wan swallowed. "What's the bad news?"

"It's set to blow in three minutes," Qui-Gon said. "I need fifteen."

Obi-Wan felt seconds tick by, precious seconds, while he absorbed this. To have come this far and have Xanatos win! He could not let it happen.

"His hatred has led him to destroy a planet just to destroy me," Qui-Gon mused. "Not to mention a sizeable fortune. VeerTa said the wealth of the ionite vein alone is immeasurable."

"Ionite?" Obi-Wan asked. "I thought this was an azurite mine."

"They found a vein after the explosion," Qui-Gon said. "The force blew rocks upward from the core." He gestured down the tunnel.

"Does the bomb have a clock?" Obi-Wan asked.

Qui-Gon nodded. "An ion clock. Precise to the second. Why?"

Obi-Wan didn't answer. He flew down the tunnel, toward the pile of debris. He picked up a rock and scraped a fingernail against it. He saw the glow of ionite. He picked up more rocks, stacking them into his tunic.

"One minute left," Qui-Gon called.

"We're not dead yet," Obi-Wan answered, running back to him. He placed the rocks carefully around the bomb.

"What are . . . ?" Qui-Gon's question died on his lips. The digital readout had stopped functioning. "What —"

"Ionite," Obi-Wan said. "It has a neutral charge. Makes most instruments stop dead. Especially timers. Miners fear it, but now, it will save them." He grinned. "You've got your fifteen minutes, Qui-Gon."

Qui-Gon blew out a long breath. "Then I'd better get started," he said.

CHAPTER 19

Covered with grime, their tunics stiff with sweat, the Jedi wearily made their way to the governor's palace. There, they found SonTag in conference with VeerTa and Clat'Ha.

"There was an emergency evacuation at the mine," SonTag told them, frowning worriedly. "Yet our sensors show nothing wrong."

"We just replaced and double-checked them yesterday," Clat'Ha put in.

"And we received word that Offworld had a problem on their deepsea mining platform," VeerTa added. "The miners' electro-collars all malfunctioned. They revolted and abandoned the mine. Their leader — a Phindian named Guerra — said to tell you he's okay."

Obi-Wan felt a glow of satisfaction. Guerra was free.

"Not that we sympathize with Offworld," Clat'Ha added. "It's a good thing. Those miners were slaves. But why are we all having sensor malfunction?"

"Equipment failure is not your problem," Qui-Gon told them. "I'm afraid I have a more painful failure to reveal."

Quickly, Qui-Gon told them what had happened at the mine.

"So Xanatos *was* behind the first explosion," SonTag said, grief in her face. "If only we hadn't trusted him!"

"I knew we shouldn't have!" VeerTa announced, her eyes flashing.

Clat'Ha simply watched Qui-Gon. "What do you mean when you say you must reveal a more painful failure?" she asked.

Leave it to Clat'Ha to jump to the next step, Qui-Gon thought admiringly. "Someone close to you has betrayed you," he said. "Someone was in league with Xanatos. They betrayed Bandomeer for personal gain and told him about the ionite."

VeerTa went pale. "But who would do such a thing?"

Qui-Gon let his gaze remain on her. Slowly, her paleness was replaced with a flush of color.

Clat'Ha turned to her. "VeerTa?"

"It was for the good of Bandomeer!" VeerTa cried. "That's what he told me. If Offworld was secretly behind the Home Planet Mine, it would be sure to be profitable."

"Did you really think that he would allow us to own the mine?" Clat'Ha asked her furiously.

"There is something else," Qui-Gon said. "Xanatos had a back-up plan. He wanted to blow up most of Bandomeer. Those black boxes were planted next to explosives in all the Enrichment Zones, plus the mining platforms. Somebody helped him smuggle those boxes into the domes."

"He said it was mining equipment for future operations," VeerTa whispered.

"Bandomeer was almost destroyed," SonTag said, her voice as sharp as the edge of a vibroblade. "If it weren't for the Jedi . . ."

"There was no way I could have known!" VeerTa cried. "Why would Xanatos destroy Bandomeer? He would destroy his own profits!"

Qui-Gon said nothing. He knew that if there was one thing stronger than greed, it was revenge. Xanatos had plotted for this very day. He had used VeerTa. He knew that Qui-Gon would die knowing he had been unable to save countless lives. It was the most painful death Xanatos could arrange for him.

Qui-Gon had underestimated Xanatos once again. He had not realized that his former apprentice was just as much a slave to the past as he was.

No, Qui-Gon corrected. His own past would no longer hold him hostage. He would leave it on Bandomeer.

Clat'Ha rose and moved away stiffly, as if she couldn't breathe the same air as VeerTa. "Where is Xanatos now?" she asked Qui-Gon.

"He has escaped," Obi-Wan reported. "His plans were already arranged; he thought he would be leaving a destroyed planet."

"Perhaps he is at Offworld's home base," VeerTa said.

Clat'Ha shot her a look of disgust. "No one knows where that is. Mark this, VeerTa. You will pay for your crime. Your friend will not."

"Yes," Qui-Gon said softly, "he will."

Qui-Gon and Obi-Wan returned to their chamber to gather their belongings. There was a transport ship leaving in a few hours.

"Yoda has another mission for us," Qui-Gon explained to Obi-Wan.

Us. Obi-Wan felt a thrill at the word.

Qui-Gon stood unmoving, staring down at his sleep-couch. A piece of paper had been stabbed to the cushion with a vibro-shiv. Obi-Wan crossed the room to read over Qui-Gon's broad shoulder:

If you are reading this, I suppose I underesti-mated you. I won't next time. I enjoyed our ad-venture together, Master. I am certain you will have the pleasure of meeting me again.

Obi-Wan couldn't read his Master's features. He tested the Force, searching for the waves of Qui-Gon's anger. He felt nothing. Was Qui-Gon containing his anger, shielding Obi-Wan, once again, from his emotions?

"I'm not angry, Obi-Wan," Qui-Gon said. "Xanatos is gone from me. He is just another enemy now. The hate is all on his side. I am pre-pared to fight the evil he does. He may kill me one day, but he will never wound me again."

Qui-Gon turned. "You showed me this. In the mine, when you reached out with the Force and showed me how light can always battle dark. My anger left me. In the end, you taught me something about myself. And when the Pad-awan teaches a Master in turn, the partnership is right."

"You called me Padawan in the mine," Obi-Wan said hopefully.

"You would have died for me," Qui-Gon said. "Your courage was extraordinary, even for a Jedi. I would be honored to accept you as my Padawan, Obi-Wan Kenobi."

Obi-Wan felt warmth fill him. He didn't feel the pride he thought he'd feel, hearing those words. But the Force moved around him and in him, and he felt a deep sense of home. He swallowed. "I accept, Master, Qui-Gon Jinn."

"Of course," Qui-Gon added, "you would not have succeeded with your plan. I would have stopped you from dying for me."

"You would not have been able to, Master," Obi-Wan replied serenely.

They exchanged a look, half-challenge, half-amusement. The Force pulsed between them. Both of them saw ahead to the long years and many missions to come. They knew they would debate this over those years, even as the memory of a planet called Bandomeer had faded. It would be a friendly disagreement between them, a bond of history and trust.

They smiled in recognition. Shared thought was one of the first bonding steps between Master and Padawan. It let them know they were on a path together. They would stride toward a future, forged from their shared past.

Qui-Gon put a hand on Obi-Wan's shoulder and rested it there.

"We'd better pack," he said quietly. "We have a long way to go."